Tales of St. Austin's

P. G. Wodehouse

Tales of St. Austin's

ISBN: 978-1-64799-326-9

PREFACE

Most of these stories originally appeared in The Captain. I am indebted to the Editor of that magazine for allowing me to republish. The rest are from the Public School Magazine. The story entitled 'A Shocking Affair' appears in print for the first time. 'This was one of our failures.'

P. G. Wodehouse

CONTENTS

1

HOW PILLINGSHOT SCORED

Pillingshot was annoyed. He was disgusted, mortified; no other word for it. He had no objection, of course, to Mr. Mellish saying that his work during the term, and especially his Livy, had been disgraceful. A master has the right to say that sort of thing if he likes. It is one of the perquisites of the position. But when he went on to observe, without a touch of shame, that there would be an examination in the Livy as far as they had gone in it on the following Saturday, Pillingshot felt that he exceeded. It was not playing the game. There were the examinations at the end of term. Those were fair enough. You knew exactly when they were coming, and could make your arrangements accordingly. But to spring an examination on you in the middle of the term out of a blue sky, as it were, was underhand and unsportsmanlike, and would not do at all. Pillingshot wished that he could put his foot down. He would have liked to have stalked up to Mr. Mellish's desk, fixed him with a blazing eye, and remarked, 'Sir, withdraw that remark. Cancel that statement instantly, or—!' or words to that effect.

What he did say was: 'Oo, si-i-r!!'

'Yes,' said Mr. Mellish, not troubling to conceal his triumph at Pillingshot's reception of the news, 'there will be a Livy examination next Saturday. And—' (he almost intoned this last observation)— 'anybody who does not get fifty per cent, Pillingshot, fifty per cent, will be severely punished. Very severely punished, Pillingshot.'

After which the lesson had proceeded on its course.

'Yes, it is rather low, isn't it?' said Pillingshot's friend, Parker, as Pillingshot came to the end of a stirring excursus on the rights of the citizen, with special reference to mid-term Livy examinations. 'That's the worst of Mellish. He always has you somehow.'

'But what am I to do?' raved Pillingshot.

'I should advise you to swot it up before Saturday,' said Parker.

'Oh, don't be an ass,' said Pillingshot, irritably.

What was the good of friends if they could only make idiotic suggestions like that?

He retired, brooding, to his house.

The day was Wednesday. There were only two more days,

therefore, in which to prepare a quarter of a book of Livy. It couldn't be done. The thing was not possible.

In the house he met Smythe.

'What are you going to do about it?' he inquired. Smythe was top of the form, and if he didn't know how to grapple with a crisis of this sort, who could know?

'If you'll kindly explain,' said Smythe, 'what the dickens you are talking about, I might be able to tell you.'

Pillingshot explained, with unwonted politeness, that 'it' meant the Livy examination.

'Oh,' said Smythe, airily, 'that! I'm just going to skim through it in case I've forgotten any of it. Then I shall read up the notes carefully. And then, if I have time, I shall have a look at the history of the period. I should advise you to do that, too.'

'Oh, don't be a goat,' said Pillingshot.

And he retired, brooding, as before.

That afternoon he spent industriously, copying out the fourth book of The Aeneid. At the beginning of the week he had had a slight disagreement with M. Gerard, the French master.

Pillingshot's views on behaviour and deportment during French lessons did not coincide with those of M. Gerard. Pillingshot's idea of a French lesson was something between a pantomime rally and a scrum at football. To him there was something wonderfully entertaining in the process of 'barging' the end man off the edge of the form into space, and upsetting his books over him. M. Gerard, however, had a very undeveloped sense of humour. He warned the humorist twice, and on the thing happening a third time, suggested that he should go into extra lesson on the ensuing Wednesday.

So Pillingshot went, and copied out Virgil.

He emerged from the room of detention at a quarter past four. As he came out into the grounds he espied in the middle distance somebody being carried on a stretcher in the direction of the School House. At the same moment Parker loomed in sight, walking swiftly towards the School shop, his mobile features shining with the rapt expression of one who sees much ginger-beer in the near future.

'Hullo, Parker,' said Pillingshot, 'who's the corpse?'

'What, haven't you heard?' said Parker. 'Oh, no, of course, you were in extra. It's young Brown. He's stunned or something.'

'How did it happen?'

'That rotter, Babington, in Dacre's. Simply slamming about, you know, getting his eye in before going in, and Brown walked slap into one of his drives. Got him on the side of the head.'

'Much hurt?'

'Oh, no, I don't think so. Keep him out of school for about a week.'

'Lucky beast. Wish somebody would come and hit me on the head. Come and hit me on the head, Parker.'

'Come and have an ice,' said Parker.

'Right-ho,' said Pillingshot. It was one of his peculiarities, that whatever the hour or the state of the weather, he was always equal to consuming an ice. This was probably due to genius. He had an infinite capacity for taking pains. Scarcely was he outside the promised ice when another misfortune came upon him. Scott, of the First Eleven, entered the shop. Pillingshot liked Scott, but he was not blind to certain flaws in the latter's character. For one thing, he was too energetic. For another, he could not keep his energy to himself. He was always making Pillingshot do things. And Pillingshot's notion of the ideal life was complete dolce far niente.

'Ginger-beer, please,' said Scott, with parched lips. He had been bowling at the nets, and the day was hot. 'Hullo! Pillingshot, you young slacker, why aren't you changed? Been bunking half-holiday games? You'd better reform, young man.'

'I've been in extra,' said Pillingshot, with dignity.

'How many times does that make this term? You're going for the record, aren't you? Jolly sporting of you. Bit slow in there, wasn't it? 'Nother ginger-beer, please.'

'Just a bit,' said Pillingshot.

'I thought so. And now you're dying for some excitement. Of course you are. Well, cut over to the House and change, and then come back and field at the nets. The man Yorke is going to bowl me some of his celebrated slow tosh, and I'm going to show him exactly how Jessop does it when he's in form.'

Scott was the biggest hitter in the School. Mr. Yorke was one of the masters. He bowled slow leg-breaks, mostly half-volleys and long hops. Pillingshot had a sort of instinctive idea that fielding out in the deep with Mr. Yorke bowling and Scott batting would not contribute largely to the gaiety of his afternoon. Fielding deep at the nets meant that you stood in the middle of the football field, where there was no telling what a ball would do if it came at you along the ground. If you were lucky you escaped without injury. Generally, however, the ball bumped and deprived you of wind or teeth, according to the height to which it rose. He began politely, but firmly, to excuse himself.

'Don't talk rot,' said Scott, complainingly, 'you must have some exercise or you'll go getting fat. Think what a blow it would be to your family, Pillingshot, if you lost your figure. Buck up. If you're back here in a quarter of an hour you shall have another ice. A large ice, Pillingshot, price sixpence. Think of it.'

The word ice, as has been remarked before, touched chords in Pillingshot's nature to which he never turned a deaf ear. Within the prescribed quarter of an hour he was back again, changed.

'Here's the ice,' said Scott, 'I've been keeping it warm for you. Shovel it down. I want to be starting for the nets. Quicker, man, quicker! Don't roll it round your tongue as if it was port. Go for it. Finished? That's right. Come on.'

Pillingshot had not finished, but Scott so evidently believed that he had, that it would have been unkind to have mentioned the fact. He followed the smiter to the nets.

If Pillingshot had passed the earlier part of the afternoon in a sedentary fashion, he made up for it now. Scott was in rare form, and Pillingshot noticed with no small interest that, while he invariably hit Mr. Yorke's deliveries a quarter of a mile or so, he never hit two balls in succession in the same direction. As soon as the panting fieldsman had sprinted to one side of the football ground and returned the ball, there was a beautiful, musical plonk, and the ball soared to the very opposite quarter of the field. It was a fine exhibition of hitting, but Pillingshot felt that he would have enjoyed it more if he could have watched it from a deck-chair.

'You're coming on as a deep field, young Pillingshot,' said Scott, as he took off his pads. 'You've got a knack of stopping them with your stomach, which the best first-class fields never have. You ought to give lessons at it. Now we'll go and have some tea.'

If Pillingshot had had a more intimate acquaintance with the classics, he would have observed at this point, 'Timeo Danaos', and made a last dash for liberty in the direction of the shop. But he was deceived by the specious nature of Scott's remark. Visions rose before his eyes of sitting back in one of Scott's armchairs, watching a fag toasting muffins, which he would eventually dispatch with languid enjoyment. So he followed Scott to his study. The classical parallel to his situation is the well-known case of the oysters. They, too, were eager for the treat.

They had reached the study, and Pillingshot was about to fling himself, with a sigh of relief, into the most comfortable chair, when Scott unmasked his batteries.

'Oh, by the way,' he said, with a coolness which to Pillingshot appeared simply brazen, 'I'm afraid my fag won't be here today. The young crock's gone and got mumps, or the plague, or something. So would you mind just lighting that stove? It'll be rather warm, but that won't matter. There are some muffins in the cupboard. You might weigh in with them. You'll find the toasting-fork on the wall somewhere. It's hanging up. Got it? Good man. Fire away.'

And Scott collected five cushions, two chairs, and a tin of mixed biscuits, and made himself comfortable. Pillingshot, with feelings too deep for words (in the then limited state of his vocabulary), did as he was requested. There was something remarkable about the way Scott could always get people to do things for him. He seemed to take everything for granted. If he had had occasion to hire an assassin to make away with the German Emperor, he would have said, 'Oh, I say, you might run over to Germany and kill the Kaiser, will you, there's a good chap? Don't be long.' And he would have taken a seat and waited, without the least doubt in his mind that the thing would be carried through as desired.

Pillingshot had just finished toasting the muffins, when the door opened, and Venables, of Merevale's, came in.

'I thought I heard you say something about tea this afternoon, Scott,' said Venables. 'I just looked in on the chance. Good Heavens, man! Fancy muffins at this time of year! Do you happen to know what the thermometer is in the shade?'

'Take a seat,' said Scott. 'I attribute my entire success in life to the fact that I never find it too hot to eat muffins. Do you know Pillingshot? One of the hottest fieldsmen in the School. At least, he was just now. He's probably cooled off since then. Venables— Pillingshot, and vice versa. Buck up with the tea, Pillingshot. What, ready? Good man. Now we might almost begin.'

'Beastly thing that accident of young Brown's, wasn't it?' said Scott. 'Chaps oughtn't to go slamming about like that with the field full of fellows. I suppose he won't be right by next Saturday?'

'Not a chance. Why? Oh, yes, I forgot. He was to have scored for the team at Windybury, wasn't he?'

'Who are you going to get now?'

Venables was captain of the St Austin's team. The match next Saturday was at Windybury, on the latter's ground.

'I haven't settled,' said Venables. 'But it's easy to get somebody. Scoring isn't one of those things which only one chap in a hundred understands.'

Then Pillingshot had an idea—a great, luminous idea.

'May I score?' he asked, and waited trembling with apprehension lest the request be refused.

'All right,' said Venables, 'I don't see any reason why you shouldn't. We have to catch the 8.14 at the station. Don't you go missing it or anything.'

5

'Rather not,' said Pillingshot. 'Not much.'

On Saturday morning, at exactly 9.15, Mr. Mellish distributed the Livy papers. When he arrived at Pillingshot's seat and found it empty, an expression passed over his face like unto that of the baffled villain in transpontine melodrama.

'Where is Pillingshot?' he demanded tragically. 'Where is he?'

'He's gone with the team to Windybury, sir,' said Parker, struggling to conceal a large size in grins. 'He's going to score.'

'No,' said Mr. Mellish sadly to himself, 'he has scored.'

THE ODD TRICK

The attitude of Philip St H. Harrison, of Merevale's House, towards his fellow-man was outwardly one of genial and even sympathetic toleration. Did his form-master intimate that his conduct was not his idea of what Young England's conduct should be, P. St H. Harrison agreed cheerfully with every word he said, warmly approved his intention of laying the matter before the Headmaster, and accepted his punishment with the air of a waiter booking an order for a chump chop and fried potatoes. But the next day there would be a squeaking desk in the form-room, just to show the master that he had not been forgotten. Or, again, did the captain of his side at football speak rudely to him on the subject of kicking the ball through in the scrum, Harrison would smile gently, and at the earliest opportunity tread heavily on the captain's toe. In short, he was a youth who made a practice of taking very good care of himself. Yet he had his failures. The affair of Graham's mackintosh was one of them, and it affords an excellent example of the truth of the proverb that a cobbler should stick to his last. Harrison's forte was diplomacy. When he forsook the arts of the diplomatist for those of the brigand, he naturally went wrong. And the manner of these things was thus.

Tony Graham was a prefect in Merevale's, and part of his duties was to look after the dormitory of which Harrison was one of the ornaments. It was a dormitory that required a good deal of keeping in order. Such choice spirits as Braithwaite of the Upper Fourth, and Mace, who was rapidly driving the master of the Lower Fifth into a premature grave, needed a firm hand. Indeed, they generally needed not only a firm hand, but a firm hand grasping a serviceable walking-stick. Add to these Harrison himself, and others of a similar calibre, and it will be seen that Graham's post was no sinecure. It was Harrison's custom to throw off his mask at night with his other garments, and appear in his true character of an abandoned villain, willing to stick at nothing as long as he could do it strictly incog. In this capacity he had come into constant contact with Graham. Even in the dark it is occasionally possible for a prefect to tell where a noise comes from. And if the said prefect has been harassed six days in the week by a noise, and locates it suddenly on the seventh, it is wont to be bad for the producer and patentee of same.

And so it came about that Harrison, enjoying himself one night, after the manner of his kind, was suddenly dropped upon with violence. He had constructed an ingenious machine, consisting of a biscuit tin, some pebbles, and some string. He put the pebbles in the tin, tied the string to it, and placed it under a chest of drawers. Then he took the other end of the string to bed with him, and settled down to make a night of it. At first all went well. Repeated inquiries from Tony failed to produce the author of the disturbance, and when finally the questions ceased, and the prefect appeared to have given the matter up as a bad job, P. St H. Harrison began to feel that under certain circumstances life was worth living. It was while he was in this happy frame of mind that the string, with which he had just produced a triumphant rattle from beneath the chest of drawers, was seized, and the next instant its owner was enjoying the warmest minute of a chequered career. Tony, like Brer Rabbit, had laid low until he was certain of the direction from which the sound proceeded. He had then slipped out of bed, crawled across the floor in a snake-like manner which would have done credit to a Red Indian, found the tin, and traced the string to its owner. Harrison emerged from the encounter feeling sore and unfit for any further recreation. This deed of the night left its impression on Harrison. The account had to be squared somehow, and in a few days his chance came. Merevale's were playing a 'friendly' with the School House, and in default of anybody better, Harrison had been pressed into service as umpire. This in itself had annoyed him. Cricket was not in his line—he was not one of your flannelled fools— and of all things in connection with the game he loathed umpiring most.

When, however, Tony came on to bowl at his end, vice Charteris, who had been hit for three fours in an over by Scott, the School slogger, he recognized that even umpiring had its advantages, and resolved to make the most of the situation.

Scott had the bowling, and he lashed out at Tony's first ball in his usual reckless style. There was an audible click, and what the sporting papers call confident appeals came simultaneously from Welch, Merevale's captain, who was keeping wicket, and Tony himself. Even Scott seemed to know that his time had come. He moved a step or two away from the wicket, but stopped before going farther to look at the umpire, on the off-chance of a miracle happening to turn his decision in the batsman's favour.

The miracle happened.

8

'Not out,' said Harrison.

'Awfully curious,' he added genially to Tony, 'how like a bat those bits of grass sound! You have to be jolly smart to know where a noise comes from, don't you!'

Tony grunted disgustedly, and walked back again to the beginning of his run.

If ever, in the whole history of cricket, a man was out leg-before-wicket, Scott was so out to Tony's second ball. It was hardly worth appealing for such a certainty. Still, the formality had to be gone through.

'How was that?' inquired Tony.

'Not out. It's an awful pity, don't you think, that they don't bring in that new leg-before rule?'

'Seems to me,' said Tony bitterly, 'the old rule holds pretty good when a man's leg's bang in front.'

'Rather. But you see the ball didn't pitch straight, and the rule says—'

'Oh, all right,' said Tony.

The next ball Scott hit for four, and the next after that for a couple. The fifth was a yorker, and just grazed the leg stump. The sixth was a beauty. You could see it was going to beat the batsman from the moment it left Tony's hand. Harrison saw it perfectly.

'No ball,' he shouted. And just as he spoke Scott's off-stump ricocheted towards the wicket-keeper.

'Heavens, man,' said Tony, fairly roused out of his cricket manners, a very unusual thing for him. 'I'll swear my foot never went over the crease. Look, there's the mark.'

'Rather not. Only, you see, it seemed to me you chucked that time. Of course, I know you didn't mean to, and all that sort of thing, but still, the rules—'

Tony would probably have liked to have said something very forcible about the rules at this point, but it occurred to him that after all Harrison was only within his rights, and that it was bad form to dispute the umpire's decision. Harrison walked off towards square-leg with a holy joy.

But he was too much of an artist to overdo the thing. Tony's next over passed off without interference. Possibly, however, this was because it was a very bad one. After the third over he asked Welch if he could get somebody else to umpire, as he had work to do. Welch heaved a sigh of relief, and agreed readily.

'Conscientious sort of chap that umpire of yours,' said Scott to Tony, after the match. Scott had made a hundred and four, and was feeling pleased. 'Considering he's in your House, he's awfully fair.'

9

'You mean that we generally swindle, I suppose?'

'Of course not, you rotter. You know what I mean. But, I say, that catch Welch and you appealed for must have been a near thing. I could have sworn I hit it.'

'Of course you did. It was clean out. So was the lbw. I say, did you think that ball that bowled you was a chuck? That one in my first over, you know.'

'Chuck! My dear Tony, you don't mean to say that man pulled you up for chucking? I thought your foot must have gone over the crease.'

'I believe the chap's mad,' said Tony.

'Perhaps he's taking it out of you this way for treading on his corns somehow. Have you been milling with this gentle youth lately?'

'By Jove,' said Tony, 'you're right. I gave him beans only the other night for ragging in the dormitory.'

Scott laughed.

'Well, he seems to have been getting a bit of his own back today. Lucky the game was only a friendly. Why will you let your angry passions rise, Tony? You've wrecked your analysis by it, though it's improved my average considerably. I don't know if that's any solid satisfaction to you.'

'It isn't.'

'You don't say so! Well, so long. If I were you, I should keep an eye on that conscientious umpire.'

'I will,' said Tony. 'Good-night.'

The process of keeping an eye on Harrison brought no results. When he wished to behave himself well, he could. On such occasions Sandford and Merton were literally not in it with him, and the hero of a Sunday-school story would simply have refused to compete. But Nemesis, as the poets tell us, though no sprinter, manages, like the celebrated Maisie, to get right there in time. Give her time, and she will arrive. She arrived in the case of Harrison. One morning, about a fortnight after the House-match incident, Harrison awoke with a new sensation. At first he could not tell what exactly this sensation was, and being too sleepy to discuss nice points of internal emotion with himself, was just turning over with the intention of going to sleep again, when the truth flashed upon him. The sensation he felt was loneliness, and the reason he felt lonely was because he was the only occupant of the dormitory. To right and left and all around were empty beds.

As he mused drowsily on these portents, the distant sound of a bell came to his ears and completed the cure. It was the bell for chapel. He dragged his watch from under his pillow, and looked at it with consternation. Four minutes to seven. And chapel was at seven. Now Harrison had been late for chapel before. It was not the thought of missing the service that worried him. What really was serious was that he had been late so many times before that Merevale had hinted at serious steps to be taken if he were late again, or, at any rate, until a considerable interval of punctuality had elapsed.

That threat had been uttered only yesterday, and here he was in all probability late once more.

There was no time to dress. He sprang out of bed, passed a sponge over his face as a concession to the decencies, and looked round for something to cover his night-shirt, which, however suitable for dormitory use, was, he felt instinctively, scarcely the garment to wear in public.

Fate seemed to fight for him. On one of the pegs in the wall hung a mackintosh, a large, blessed mackintosh. He was inside it in a moment.

Four minutes later he rushed into his place in chapel.

The short service gave him some time for recovering himself. He left the building feeling a new man. His costume, though quaint, would not call for comment. Chapel at St Austin's was never a full-dress ceremony. Mackintoshes covering night-shirts were the rule rather than the exception.

But between his costume and that of the rest there was this subtle distinction. They wore their own mackintoshes. He wore somebody else's.

The bulk of the School had split up into sections, each section making for its own House, and Merevale's was already in sight, when Harrison felt himself grasped from behind. He turned, to see Graham.

'Might I ask,' enquired Tony with great politeness, 'who said you might wear my mackintosh?'

Harrison gasped.

'I suppose you didn't know it was mine?'

'No, no, rather not. I didn't know.'

'And if you had known it was mine, you wouldn't have taken it, I suppose?'

'Oh no, of course not,' said Harrison. Graham seemed to be taking an unexpectedly sensible view of the situation.

'Well,' said Tony, 'now that you know that it is mine, suppose you give it up.'

'Give it up!'

11

'Yes; buck up. It looks like rain, and I mustn't catch cold.'

'But, Graham, I've only got on—'

'Spare us these delicate details. Mack up, please, I want it.'

Finally, Harrison appearing to be difficult in the matter, Tony took the garment off for him, and went on his way.

Harrison watched him go with mixed feelings. Righteous indignation struggled with the gravest apprehension regarding his own future. If Merevale should see him! Horrible thought. He ran. He had just reached the House, and was congratulating himself on having escaped, when the worst happened. At the private entrance stood Merevale, and with him the Headmaster himself. They both eyed him with considerable interest as he shot in at the boys' entrance.

'Harrison,' said Merevale after breakfast.

'Yes, sir?'

'The Headmaster wishes to see you—again.'

'Yes, sir,' said Harrison.

There was a curious lack of enthusiasm in his voice.

3

L'AFFAIRE UNCLE JOHN

(A Story in Letters)

I

From Richard Venables, of St Austin's School, to his brother Archibald Venables, of King's College, Cambridge:

Dear Archie—I take up my pen to write to you, not as one hoping for an answer, but rather in order that (you notice the Thucydidean construction) I may tell you of an event the most important of those that have gone before. You may or may not have heard far-off echoes of my adventure with Uncle John, who has just come back from the diamond-mines—and looks it. It happened thusly:

Last Wednesday evening I was going through the cricket field to meet Uncle John, at the station, as per esteemed favour from the governor, telling me to. Just as I got on the scene, to my horror, amazement, and disgust, I saw a middle-aged bounder, in loud checks, who, from his looks, might have been anything from a retired pawnbroker to a second-hand butler, sacked from his last place for stealing the sherry, standing in the middle of the field, on the very wicket the Rugborough match is to be played on next Saturday (tomorrow), and digging—digging—I'll trouble you. Excavating great chunks of our best turf with a walking-stick. I was so unnerved, I nearly fainted. It's bad enough being captain of a School team under any circs., as far as putting you off your game goes, but when you see the wicket you've been rolling by day, and dreaming about by night, being mangled by an utter stranger—well! They say a cow is slightly irritated when her calf is taken away from her, but I don't suppose the most maternal cow that ever lived came anywhere near the frenzy that surged up in my bosom at that moment. I flew up to him, foaming at the mouth. 'My dear sir,' I shrieked, 'are you aware that you're spoiling the best wicket that has ever been prepared since cricket began?' He looked at me, in a dazed sort of way, and said, 'What?' I said: 'How on earth do you think we're going to play Rugborough on a ploughed field?' 'I don't

13

follow, mister,' he replied. A man who calls you 'mister' is beyond the pale. You are justified in being a little rude to him. So I said: 'Then you must be either drunk or mad, and I trust it's the latter.' I believe that's from some book, though I don't remember which. This did seem to wake him up a bit, but before he could frame his opinion in words, up came Biffen, the ground-man, to have a last look at his wicket before retiring for the night. When he saw the holes—they were about a foot deep, and scattered promiscuously, just where two balls out of three pitch—he almost had hysterics. I gently explained the situation to him, and left him to settle with my friend of the check suit. Biffen was just settling down to a sort of Philippic when I went, and I knew that I had left the man in competent hands. Then I went to the station. The train I had been told to meet was the 5.30. By the way, of course, I didn't know in the least what Uncle John was like, not having seen him since I was about one-and-a-half, but I had been told to look out for a tall, rather good-looking man. Well, the 5.30 came in all right, but none of the passengers seemed to answer to the description. The ones who were tall were not good looking, and the only man who was good looking stood five feet nothing in his boots. I did ask him if he was Mr. John Dalgliesh; but, his name happening to be Robinson, he could not oblige. I sat out a couple more trains, and then went back to the field. The man had gone, but Biffen was still there. 'Was you expecting anyone today, sir?' he asked, as I came up. 'Yes. Why?' I said. 'That was 'im,' said Biffen. By skilful questioning, I elicited the whole thing. It seems that the fearsome bargee, in checks, was the governor's 'tall, good-looking man'; in other words, Uncle John himself. He had come by the 4.30, I suppose. Anyway, there he was, and I had insulted him badly. Biffen told me that he had asked who I was, and that he (Biffen) had given the information, while he was thinking of something else to say to him about his digging. By the way, I suppose he dug from force of habit. Thought he'd find diamonds, perhaps. When Biffen told him this, he said in a nasty voice: 'Then, when he comes back will you have the goodness to tell him that my name is John Dalgliesh, and that he will hear more of this.' And I'm uncommonly afraid I shall. The governor bars Uncle John awfully, I know, but he wanted me to be particularly civil to him, because he was to get me a place in some beastly firm when I leave. I haven't heard from home yet, but I expect to soon. Still, I'd like to know how I could stand and watch him ruining the wicket for our spot match of the season. As it is, it won't be as good as it would have been. The Rugborough slow man

14

will be unplayable if he can find one of these spots. Altogether, it's a beastly business. Write soon, though I know you won't—Yours ever, Dick.

II

Telegram from Major-General Sir Everard Venables, V.C., K.C.M.G., to his son Richard Venables:

Venables, St Austin's. What all this about Uncle John. Says were grossly rude. Write explanation next post—Venables.

III

Letter from Mr.s James Anthony (nee Miss Dorothy Venables) to her brother Richard Venables:

Dear Dick—What have you been doing to Uncle John? Jim and I are stopping for a fortnight with father, and have just come in for the whole thing. Uncle John—isn't he a horrible man?—says you were grossly insolent to him when he went down to see you. Do write and tell me all about it. I have heard no details as yet. Father refuses to give them, and gets simply furious when the matter is mentioned. Jim said at dinner last night that a conscientious boy would probably feel bound to be rude to Uncle John. Father said 'Conscience be—'; I forget the rest, but it was awful. Jim says if he gets any worse we shall have to sit on his head, and cut the traces. He is getting so dreadfully horsey. Do write the very minute you get this. I want to know all about it.—Your affectionate sister, Dorothy

IV

PART OF LETTER FROM RICHARD VENABLES, OF ST AUSTIN'S, TO HIS FATHER

Major-General Sir Everard Venables, V.C., K.C.M.G.:
... So you see it was really his fault. The Emperor of Germany has no right to come and dig holes in our best wicket. Take a parallel case. Suppose some idiot of a fellow (not that Uncle John's that, of course, but you know what I mean) came and began rooting up your azaleas. Wouldn't you want to say something cutting? I will apologize to Uncle John, if you like; but still, I do think he might have gone somewhere else if he really wanted to dig. So you see, etc., etc.

V

Letter from Richard Venables, of St Austin's, to his sister Mr.s James Anthony:
Dear Dolly—Thanks awfully for your letter, and thank Jim for his message. He's a ripper. I'm awfully glad you married him and not that rotter, Thompson, who used to hang on so. I hope the most marvellous infant on earth is flourishing. And now about Uncle John. Really, I am jolly glad I did say all that to him. We played Rugborough yesterday, and the wicket was simply vile. They won the toss, and made two hundred and ten. Of course, the wicket was all right at one end, and that's where they made most of their runs. I was wicket-keeping as usual, and I felt awfully ashamed of the beastly pitch when their captain asked me if it was the football-field. Of course, he wouldn't have said that if he hadn't been a pal of mine,

16

but it was probably what the rest of the team thought, only they were too polite to say so. When we came to bat it was worse than ever. I went in first with Welch—that's the fellow who stopped a week at home a few years ago; I don't know whether you remember him. He got out in the first over, caught off a ball that pitched where Uncle John had been prospecting, and jumped up. It was rotten luck, of course, and worse was to follow, for by half-past five we had eight wickets down for just over the hundred, and only young Scott, who's simply a slogger, and another fellow to come in. Well, Scott came in. I had made about sixty then, and was fairly well set—and he started simply mopping up the bowling. He gave a chance every over as regular as clockwork, and it was always missed, and then he would make up for it with two or three tremendous whangs—a safe four every time. It wasn't batting. It was more like golf. Well, this went on for some time, and we began to get hopeful again, having got a hundred and eighty odd. I just kept up my wicket, while Scott hit. Then he got caught, and the last man, a fellow called Moore, came in. I'd put him in the team as a bowler, but he could bat a little, too, on occasions, and luckily this was one of them. There were only eleven to win, and I had the bowling. I was feeling awfully fit, and put their slow man clean over the screen twice running, which left us only three to get. Then it was over, and Moore played the fast man in grand style, though he didn't score. Well, I got the bowling again, and half-way through the over I carted a half-volley into the Pav., and that gave us the match. Moore hung on for a bit and made about ten, and then got bowled. We made 223 altogether, of which I had managed to get seventy-eight, not out. It pulls my average up a good bit. Rather decent, isn't it? The fellows rotted about a good deal, and chaired me into the Pav., but it was Scott who won us the match, I think. He made ninety-four. But Uncle John nearly did for us with his beastly walking-stick. On a good wicket we might have made any number. I don't know how the affair will end. Keep me posted up in the governor's symptoms, and write again soon.—Your affectionate brother, Dick

PS.—On looking over this letter, I find I have taken it for granted that you know all about the Uncle John affair. Probably you do, but, in case you don't, it was this way. You see, I was going, etc., etc.

VI

From Archibald Venables, of King's College, Cambridge, to Richard Venables, of St Austin's:

Dear Dick—Just a line to thank you for your letter, and to tell you that since I got it I have had a visit from the great Uncle John, too. He is an outsider, if you like. I gave him the best lunch I could in my rooms, and the man started a long lecture on extravagance. He doesn't seem to understand the difference between the 'Varsity and a private school. He kept on asking leading questions about pocket-money and holidays, and wanted to know if my master allowed me to walk in the streets in that waistcoat—a remark which cut me to the quick, 'that waistcoat' being quite the most posh thing of the sort in Cambridge. He then enquired after my studies; and, finally, when I saw him off at the station, said that he had decided not to tip me, because he was afraid that I was inclined to be extravagant. I was quite kind to him, however, in spite of everything; but I was glad you had spoken to him like a father. The recollection of it soothed me, though it seemed to worry him. He talked a good deal about it. Glad you came off against Rugborough.—Yours ever, A. Venables

VII

From Mr. John Dalgliesh to Mr. Philip Mortimer, of Penge:

Dear Sir—In reply to your letter of the 18th inst., I shall be happy to recommend your son, Reginald, for the vacant post in the firm of Messrs Van Nugget, Diomonde, and Mynes, African merchants. I have written them to that effect, and you will, doubtless, receive a communication from them shortly.—I am, my dear sir, yours faithfully, J. Dalgliesh

VIII

From Richard Venables, of St Austin's, to his father Major-General Sir Everard Venables, V.C., K.C.M.G.:

Dear Father—Uncle John writes, in answer to my apology, to say that no apologies will meet the case; and that he has given his nomination in that rotten City firm of his to a fellow called Mortimer. But rather a decent thing has happened. There is a chap here I know pretty well, who is the son of Lord Marmaduke Twistleton, and it appears that the dook himself was down watching the Rugborough match, and liked my batting. He came and talked to me after the match, and asked me what I was going to do when I left, and I said I wasn't certain, and he said that, if I hadn't anything better on, he could give me a place on his estate up in Scotland, as a sort of land-agent, as he wanted a chap who could play cricket, because he was keen on the game himself, and always had a lot going on in the summer up there. So he says that, if I go up to the 'Varsity for three years, he can guarantee me the place when I come down, with a jolly good screw and a ripping open-air life, with lots of riding, and so on, which is just what I've always wanted. So, can I? It's the sort of opportunity that won't occur again, and you know you always said the only reason I couldn't go up to the 'Varsity was, that it would be a waste of time. But in this case, you see, it won't, because he wants me to go, and guarantees me the place when I come down. It'll be awfully fine, if I may. I hope you'll see it.—Your affectionate son, Dick

PS.—I think he's writing to you. He asked your address. I think Uncle John's a rotter. I sent him a rattling fine apology, and this is how he treats it. But it'll be all right if you like this land-agent idea. If you like, you might wire your answer.

IX

Telegram from Major-General Sir Everard Venables, V.C., K.C.M.G., to his son Richard Venables, of St Austin's:

Venables, St Austin's. Very well.—Venables

19

X

Extract from Letter from Richard Venables, of St Austin's, to his father Major-General Sir Everard Venables, V.C., K.C.M.G.:

... Thanks, awfully—

Extract from The Austinian of October:

The following O.A.s have gone into residence this year: At Oxford, J. Scrymgeour, Corpus Christi; R. Venables, Trinity; K. Crespigny-Brown, Balliol.

Extract from the Daily Mail's account of the 'Varsity match of the following summer:

... The St Austin's freshman, Venables, fully justified his inclusion by scoring a stylish fifty-seven. He hit eight fours, and except for a miss-hit in the slips, at 51, which Smith might possibly have secured had he started sooner, gave nothing like a chance. Venables, it will be remembered, played several good innings for Oxford in the earlier matches, notably, his not out contribution of 103 against Sussex—

4

HARRISON'S SLIGHT ERROR

The one o'clock down express was just on the point of starting. The engine-driver, with his hand on the lever, whiled away the moments, like the watchman in The Agamemnon, by whistling. The guard endeavoured to talk to three people at once. Porters flitted to and fro, cleaving a path for themselves with trucks of luggage. The Usual Old Lady was asking if she was right for some place nobody had ever heard of. Everybody was saying good-bye to everybody else, and last, but not least, P. St H. Harrison, of St Austin's, was strolling at a leisurely pace towards the rear of the train. There was no need for him to hurry. For had not his friend, Mace, promised to keep a corner-seat for him while he went to the refreshment-room to lay in supplies? Undoubtedly he had, and Harrison, as he watched the struggling crowd, congratulated himself that he was not as other men. A corner seat in a carriage full of his own particular friends, with plenty of provisions, and something to read in case he got tired of talking—it would be perfect.

So engrossed was he in these reflections, that he did not notice that from the opposite end of the platform a youth of about his own age was also making for the compartment in question. The first intimation he had of his presence was when the latter, arriving first at the door by a short head, hurled a bag on to the rack, and sank gracefully into the identical corner seat which Harrison had long regarded as his own personal property. And to make matters worse, there was no other vacant seat in the compartment. Harrison was about to protest, when the guard blew his whistle. There was nothing for it but to jump in and argue the matter out en route. Harrison jumped in, to be greeted instantly by a chorus of nine male voices. 'Outside there! No room! Turn him out!' said the chorus. Then the chorus broke up into its component parts, and began to address him one by one.

'You rotter, Harrison,' said Babington, of Dacre's, 'what do you come barging in here for? Can't you see we're five aside already?'

'Hope you've brought a sardine-opener with you, old chap,' said Barrett, the peerless pride of Philpott's, "cos we shall jolly well need one when we get to the good old Junct-i-on. Get up into the rack, Harrison, you're stopping the ventilation.'

The youth who had commandeered Harrison's seat so neatly took another unpardonable liberty at this point. He grinned. Not the timid, deprecating smile of one who wishes to ingratiate himself with strangers, but a good, six-inch grin right across his face. Harrison turned on him savagely.

'Look here,' he said, 'just you get out of that. What do you mean by bagging my seat?'

'Are you a director of this line?' enquired the youth politely. Roars of applause from the interested audience. Harrison began to feel hot and uncomfortable.

'Or only the Emperor of Germany?' pursued his antagonist.

More applause, during which Harrison dropped his bag of provisions, which were instantly seized and divided on the share and share alike system, among the gratified Austinians.

'Look here, none of your cheek,' was the shockingly feeble retort which alone occurred to him. The other said nothing. Harrison returned to the attack.

'Look here,' he said, 'are you going to get out, or have I got to make you?'

Not a word did his opponent utter. To quote the bard: 'The stripling smiled.' To tell the truth, the stripling smiled inanely.

The other occupants of the carriage were far from imitating his reserve. These treacherous friends, realizing that, for those who were themselves comfortably seated, the spectacle of Harrison standing up with aching limbs for a journey of some thirty miles would be both grateful and comforting, espoused the cause of the unknown with all the vigour of which they were capable.

'Beastly bully, Harrison,' said Barrett. 'Trying to turn the kid out of his seat! Why can't you leave the chap alone? Don't you move, kid.'

'Thanks,' said the unknown, 'I wasn't going to.'

'Now you see what comes of slacking,' said Grey. 'If you'd bucked up and got here in time you might have bagged this seat I've got. By Jove, Harrison, you've no idea how comfortable it is in this corner.'

'Punctuality,' said Babington, 'is the politeness of princes.'

And again the unknown maddened Harrison with a 'best-on-record' grin.

'But, I say, you chaps,' said he, determined as a last resource to appeal to their better feelings (if any), 'Mace was keeping this seat for me, while I went to get some grub. Weren't you, Mace?' He turned to Mace for corroboration. To his surprise, Mace was nowhere to be seen.

His sympathetic school-fellows grasped the full humour of the situation as one man, and gave tongue once more in chorus.

'You weed,' they yelled joyfully, 'you've got into the wrong carriage. Mace is next door.'

And then, with the sound of unquenchable laughter ringing in his ears, Harrison gave the thing up, and relapsed into a disgusted silence. No single word did he speak until the journey was done, and the carriage emptied itself of its occupants at the Junction. The local train was in readiness to take them on to St Austin's, and this time Harrison managed to find a seat without much difficulty. But it was a bitter moment when Mace, meeting him on the platform, addressed him as a rotter, for that he had not come to claim the corner seat which he had been reserving for him. They had had, said Mace, a rattling good time coming down. What sort of a time had Harrison had in his carriage? Harrison's reply was not remarkable for its clearness.

The unknown had also entered the local train. It was plain, therefore, that he was coming to the School as a new boy. Harrison began to wonder if, under these circumstances, something might not be done in the matter by way of levelling up things. He pondered. When St Austin's station was reached, and the travellers began to stream up the road towards the College, he discovered that the newcomer was a member of his own House. He was standing close beside him, and heard Babington explaining to him the way to Merevale's. Merevale was Harrison's House-master.

It was two minutes after he had found out this fact that the Grand Idea came to Harrison. He saw his way now to a revenge so artistic, so beautifully simple, that it was with some difficulty that he restrained himself from bursting into song. For two pins, he felt, he could have done a cake-walk.

He checked his emotion. He beat it steadily back, and quenched it. When he arrived at Merevale's, he went first to the matron's room. 'Has Venables come back yet?' he asked.

Venables was the head of Merevale's House, captain of the School cricket, wing three-quarter of the School Fifteen, and a great man altogether.

'Yes,' said the matron, 'he came back early this afternoon.'

Harrison knew it. Venables always came back early on the last day of the holidays.

'He was upstairs a short while ago,' continued the matron. 'He was putting his study tidy.'

23

Harrison knew it. Venables always put his study tidy on the last day of the holidays. He took a keen and perfectly justifiable pride in his study, which was the most luxurious in the House.

'Is he there now?' asked Harrison.

'No. He has gone over to see the Headmaster.'

'Thanks,' said Harrison, 'it doesn't matter. It wasn't anything important.'

He retired triumphant. Things were going excellently well for his scheme.

His next act was to go to the fags' room, where, as he had expected, he found his friend of the train. Luck continued to be with him. The unknown was alone.

'Hullo!' said Harrison.

'Hullo!' said the fellow-traveller. He had resolved to follow Harrison's lead. If Harrison was bringing war, then war let it be. If, however, his intentions were friendly, he would be friendly too.

'I didn't know you were coming to Merevale's. It's the best House in the School.'

'Oh!'

'Yes, for one thing, everybody except the kids has a study.'

'What? Not really? Why, I thought we had to keep to this room. One of the chaps told me so.'

'Trying to green you, probably. You must look out for that sort of thing. I'll show you the way to your study, if you like. Come along upstairs.'

'Thanks, awfully. It's awfully good of you,' said the gratified unknown, and they went upstairs together.

One of the doors which they passed on their way was open, disclosing to view a room which, though bare at present, looked as if it might be made exceedingly comfortable.

'That's my den,' said Harrison. It was perhaps lucky that Graham, to whom the room belonged, in fact, as opposed to fiction, did not hear the remark. Graham and Harrison were old and tried foes. 'This is yours.' Harrison pushed open another door at the end of the passage.

His companion stared blankly at the Oriental luxury which met his eye. 'But, I say,' he said, 'are you sure? This seems to be occupied already.'

'Oh, no, that's all right,' said Harrison, airily. 'The chap who used to be here left last term. He didn't know he was going to leave till it was too late to pack up all his things, so he left his study as it was. All you've got to do is to cart the things out into the passage and leave them there. The Moke'll take 'em away.'

The Moke was the official who combined in a single body the duties of butler and bootboy at Merevale's House. 'Oh, right-ho!' said the unknown, and Harrison left him.

Harrison's idea was that when Venables returned and found an absolute stranger placidly engaged in wrecking his carefully-tidied study, he would at once, and without making inquiries, fall upon that absolute stranger and blot him off the face of the earth. Afterwards it might possibly come out that he, Harrison, had been not altogether unconnected with the business, and then, he was fain to admit, there might be trouble. But he was a youth who never took overmuch heed for the morrow. Sufficient unto the day was his motto. And, besides, it was distinctly worth risking. The main point, and the one with which alone the House would concern itself, was that he had completely taken in, scored off, and overwhelmed the youth who had done as much by him in the train, and his reputation as one not to be lightly trifled with would be restored to its former brilliance. Anything that might happen between himself and Venables subsequently would be regarded as a purely private matter between man and man, affecting the main point not at all.

About an hour later a small Merevalian informed Harrison that Venables wished to see him in his study. He went. Experience had taught him that when the Head of the House sent for him, it was as a rule as well to humour his whim and go. He was prepared for a good deal, for he had come to the conclusion that it was impossible for him to preserve his incognito in the matter, but he was certainly not prepared for what he saw.

Venables and the stranger were seated in two armchairs, apparently on the very best of terms with one another. And this, in spite of the fact that these two armchairs were the only furniture left in the study. The rest, as he had noted with a grin before he had knocked at the door, was picturesquely scattered about the passage.

'Hullo, Harrison,' said Venables, 'I wanted to see you. There seems to have been a slight mistake somewhere. Did you tell my brother to shift all the furniture out of the study?'

Harrison turned a delicate shade of green.

'Your—er—brother?' he gurgled.

'Yes. I ought to have told you my brother was coming to the Coll. this term. I told the Old Man and Merevale and the rest of the authorities. Can't make out why I forgot you. Slipped my mind somehow. However, you seem to have been doing the square thing by him, showing him round and so on. Very good of you.'

Harrison smiled feebly. Venables junior grinned. What seemed to Harrison a mystery was how the brothers had managed to arrive at the School at different times. The explanation of which was in reality very simple. The elder Venables had been spending the last week of the holidays with MacArthur, the captain of the St Austin's Fifteen, the same being a day boy, suspended within a mile of the School.

'But what I can't make out,' went on Venables, relentlessly, 'is this furniture business. To the best of my knowledge I didn't leave suddenly at the end of last term. I'll ask if you like, to make sure, but I fancy you'll find you've been mistaken. Must have been thinking of someone else. Anyhow, we thought you must know best, so we lugged all the furniture out into the passage, and now it appears there's been a mistake of sorts, and the stuff ought to be inside all the time. So would you mind putting it back again? We'd help you, only we're going out to the shop to get some tea. You might have it done by the time we get back. Thanks, awfully.'

Harrison coughed nervously, and rose to a point of order.

'I was going out to tea, too,' he said.

'I'm sorry, but I think you'll have to scratch the engagement,' said Venables.

Harrison made a last effort.

'I'm fagging for Welch this term,' he protested.

It was the rule at St Austin's that every fag had the right to refuse to serve two masters. Otherwise there would have been no peace for that down-trodden race.

'That,' said Venables, 'ought to be awfully jolly for Welch, don't you know, but as a matter of fact term hasn't begun yet. It doesn't start till tomorrow. Weigh in.'

Various feelings began to wage war beneath Harrison's Eton waistcoat. A profound disinclination to undertake the suggested task battled briskly with a feeling that, if he refused the commission, things might—nay, would—happen.

'Harrison,' said Venables gently, but with meaning, as he hesitated, 'do you know what it is to wish you had never been born?'

And Harrison, with a thoughtful expression on his face, picked up a photograph from the floor, and hung it neatly in its place over the mantelpiece.

5

BRADSHAW'S LITTLE STORY

The qualities which in later years rendered Frederick Wackerbath Bradshaw so conspicuous a figure in connection with the now celebrated affair of the European, African, and Asiatic Pork Pie and Ham Sandwich Supply Company frauds, were sufficiently in evidence during his school career to make his masters prophesy gloomily concerning his future. The boy was in every detail the father of the man. There was the same genial unscrupulousness, upon which the judge commented so bitterly during the trial, the same readiness to seize an opportunity and make the most of it, the same brilliance of tactics. Only once during those years can I remember an occasion on which Justice scored a point against him. I can remember it, because I was in a sense responsible for his failure. And he can remember it, I should be inclined to think, for other reasons. Our then Headmaster was a man with a straight eye and a good deal of muscular energy, and it is probable that the talented Frederick, in spite of the passage of years, has a tender recollection of these facts.

It was the eve of the Euripides examination in the Upper Fourth. Euripides is not difficult compared to some other authors, but he does demand a certain amount of preparation. Bradshaw was a youth who did less preparation than anybody I have ever seen, heard of, or read of, partly because he preferred to peruse a novel under the table during prep., but chiefly, I think, because he had reduced cribbing in form to such an exact science that he loved it for its own sake, and would no sooner have come tamely into school with a prepared lesson than a sportsman would shoot a sitting bird. It was not the marks that he cared for. He despised them. What he enjoyed was the refined pleasure of swindling under a master's very eye. At the trial the judge, who had, so ran report, been himself rather badly bitten by the Ham Sandwich Company, put the case briefly and neatly in the words, 'You appear to revel in villainy for villainy's sake,' and I am almost certain that I saw the beginnings of a gratified smile on Frederick's expressive face as he heard the remark. The rest of our study—the juniors at St Austin's pigged in quartettes—were in a state of considerable mental activity on account of this Euripides examination. There had been House-matches during the preceding fortnight, and House-matches are not a help to study, especially if you are on the very fringe of the cock-house team, as I was. By dint of practising every minute of spare time, I had got the eleventh place for my fielding. And, better still, I had caught two catches in the second innings, one of them a regular gallery affair, and both off the captain's bowling. It was magnificent, but it was not Euripides, and I wished now that it had been. Mellish, our form-master, had an unpleasant habit of coming down with both feet, as it were, on members of his form who failed in the book-papers.

We were working, therefore, under forced draught, and it was distinctly annoying to see the wretched Bradshaw lounging in our only armchair with one of Rider Haggard's best, seemingly quite unmoved at the prospect of Euripides examinations. For all he appeared to care, Euripides might never have written a line in his life.

Kendal voiced the opinion of the meeting.

'Bradshaw, you worm,' he said. 'Aren't you going to do any work?'

'Think not. What's the good? Can't get up a whole play of Euripides in two hours.'

'Mellish'll give you beans.'

'Let him.'

'You'll get a jolly bad report.'

'Shan't get a report at all. I always intercept it before my guardian can get it. He never says anything.'

'Mellish'll probably run you in to the Old Man,' said White, the fourth occupant of the study.

Bradshaw turned on us with a wearied air.

'Oh, do give us a rest,' he said. 'Here you are just going to do a most important exam., and you sit jawing away as if you were paid for it. Oh, I say, by the way, who's setting the paper tomorrow?'

'Mellish, of course,' said White.

'No, he isn't,' I said. 'Shows what a lot you know about it. Mellish is setting the Livy paper.'

'Then, who's doing this one?' asked Bradshaw.

'Yorke.'

Yorke was the master of the Upper Fifth. He generally set one of the upper fourth book-papers.

'Certain?' said Bradshaw.

'Absolutely.'

'Thanks. That's all I wanted to know. By Jove, I advise you chaps to read this. It's grand. Shall I read out this bit about a fight?'

'No!' we shouted virtuously, all together, though we were dying to hear it, and we turned once more to the loathsome inanities of the second chorus. If we had been doing Homer, we should have felt more in touch with Bradshaw. There's a good deal of similarity, when you come to compare them, between Homer and Haggard. They both deal largely in bloodshed, for instance. As events proved, the Euripides paper, like many things which seem formidable at a distance, was not nearly so bad as I had expected. I did a fair-to-moderate paper, and Kendal and White both seemed satisfied with themselves. Bradshaw confessed without emotion that he had only attempted the last half of the last question, and on being pressed for further information, merely laughed mysteriously, and said vaguely that it would be all right.

It now became plain that he had something up his sleeve. We expressed a unanimous desire to know what it was.

'You might tell a chap,' I said.

'Out with it, Bradshaw, or we'll lynch you,' added Kendal.

Bradshaw, however, was not to be drawn. Much of his success in the paths of crime, both at school and afterwards, was due to his secretive habits. He never permitted accomplices.

On the following Wednesday the marks were read out. Out of a possible hundred I had obtained sixty—which pleased me very much indeed—White, fifty-five, Kendal, sixty-one. The unspeakable Bradshaw's net total was four.

Mellish always read out bad marks in a hushed voice, expressive of disgust and horror, but four per cent was too much for him. He shouted it, and the form yelled applause, until Ponsonby came in from the Upper Fifth next door with Mr. Yorke's compliments, 'and would we recollect that his form were trying to do an examination'.

When order had been restored, Mellish settled his glasses and glared through them at Bradshaw, who, it may be remarked, had not turned a hair.

'Bradshaw,' he said, 'how do you explain this?'

It was merely a sighting shot, so to speak. Nobody was ever expected to answer the question. Bradshaw, however, proved himself the exception to the rule.

'I can explain, sir,' he said, 'if I may speak to you privately afterwards.'

I have seldom seen anyone so astonished as Mellish was at these words. In the whole course of his professional experience, he had never met with a parallel case. It was hard on the poor man not to be allowed to speak his mind about a matter of four per cent in a book-paper, but what could he do? He could not proceed with his denunciation, for if Bradshaw's explanation turned out a sufficient excuse, he would have to withdraw it all again, and vast stores of golden eloquence would be wasted. But, then, if he bottled up what he wished to say altogether, it might do him a serious internal injury. At last he hit on a compromise. He said, 'Very well, Bradshaw, I will hear what you have to say,' and then sprang, like the cat in the poem, 'all claws', upon an unfortunate individual who had scored twenty-nine, and who had been congratulating himself that Bradshaw's failings would act as a sort of lightning-conductor to him. Bradshaw worked off his explanation in under five minutes. I tried to stay behind to listen, on the pretext of wanting to tidy up my desk, but was ejected by request. Bradshaw explained that his statement was private.

After a time they came out together like long-lost brothers, Mellish with his hand on Bradshaw's shoulder. It was some small comfort to me to remember that Bradshaw had the greatest dislike to this sort of thing.

It was evident that Bradshaw, able exponent of the art of fiction that he was, must have excelled himself on this occasion. I tried to get the story out of him in the study that evening. White and Kendal assisted. We tried persuasion first. That having failed, we tried taunts. Then we tried kindness. Kendal sat on his legs, and I sat on his head, and White twisted his arm. I think that we should have extracted something soon, either his arm from its socket or a full confession, but we were interrupted. The door flew open, and Prater (the same being our House-master, and rather a good sort) appeared.

'Now then, now then,' he said. Prater's manner is always abrupt.

'What's this? I can't have this. I can't have this. Get up at once. Where's Bradshaw?'

I rose gracefully to my feet, thereby disclosing the classic features of the lost one.

'The Headmaster wants to see you at once, Bradshaw, at the School House. You others had better find something to do, or you will be getting into trouble.'

He and Bradshaw left together, while we speculated on the cause of the summons.

We were not left very long in suspense. In a quarter of an hour Bradshaw returned, walking painfully, and bearing what, to the expert's eye, are the unmistakable signs of a 'touching up', which, being interpreted, is corporal punishment.

'Hullo,' said White, as he appeared, 'what's all this?'

'How many?' enquired the statistically-minded Kendal. 'You'll be thankful for this when you're a man, Bradshaw.'

'That's what I always say to myself when I'm touched up,' added Kendal.

I said nothing, but it was to me that the wounded one addressed himself.

'You utter ass,' he said, in tones of concentrated venom.

'Look here, Bradshaw—' I began, protestingly.

'It's all through you—you idiot,' he snarled. 'I got twelve.'

'Twelve isn't so dusty,' said White, critically. 'Most I ever got was six.'

'But why was it?' asked Kendal. 'That's what we want to know. What have you been and gone and done?'

'It's about that Euripides paper,' said Bradshaw.

'Ah!' said Kendal.

'Yes, I don't mind telling you about it now. When Mellish had me up after school today, I'd got my yarn all ready. There wasn't a flaw in it anywhere as far as I could see. My idea was this. I told him I'd been to Yorke's room the day before the exam, to ask him if he had any marks for us. That was all right. Yorke was doing the two Unseen papers, and it was just the sort of thing a fellow would do to go and ask him about the marks.'

'Well?'

'Then when I got there he was out, and I looked about for the marks, and on the table I saw the Euripides paper.'

'By Jove!' said Kendal. We began to understand, and to realize that here was a master-mind.

'Well, of course, I read it, not knowing what it was, and then, as the only way of not taking an unfair advantage, I did as badly as I could in the exam. That was what I told Mellish. Any beak would have swallowed it.'

'Well, didn't he?'

'Mellish did all right, but the rotter couldn't keep it to himself. Went and told the Old Man. The Old Man sent for me. He was as decent as anything at first. That was just his guile. He made me describe exactly where I had seen the paper, and so on. That was rather risky, of course, but I put it as vaguely as I could. When I had finished, he suddenly whipped round, and said, "Bradshaw, why are you telling me all these lies?" That's the sort of thing that makes you feel rather a wreck. I was too surprised to say anything.'

'I can guess the rest,' said Kendal. 'But how on earth did he know it was all lies? Why didn't you stick to your yarn?'

'And, besides,' I put in, 'where do I come in? I don't see what I've got to do with it.'

Bradshaw eyed me fiercely. 'Why, the whole thing was your fault,' he said. 'You told me Yorke was setting the paper.'

'Well, so he did, didn't he?'

'No, he didn't. The Old Man set it himself,' said Bradshaw, gloomily.

6

A SHOCKING AFFAIR

The Bradshaw who appears in the following tale is the same youth who figures as the hero—or villain, label him as you like—of the preceding equally veracious narrative. I mention this because I should not care for you to go away with the idea that a waistcoat marked with the name of Bradshaw must of necessity cover a scheming heart. It may, however, be noticed that a good many members of the Bradshaw family possess a keen and rather sinister sense of the humorous, inherited doubtless from their great ancestor, the dry wag who wrote that monument of quiet drollery, Bradshaw's Railway Guide. So with the hero of my story.

Frederick Wackerbath Bradshaw was, as I have pointed out, my contemporary at St Austin's. We were in the same House, and together we sported on the green—and elsewhere—and did our best to turn the majority of the staff of masters into confirmed pessimists, they in the meantime endeavouring to do the same by us with every weapon that lay to their hand. And the worst of these weapons were the end-of-term examination papers. Mellish was our form-master, and once a term a demon entered into Mellish. He brooded silently apart from the madding crowd. He wandered through dry places seeking rest, and at intervals he would smile evilly, and jot down a note on the back of an envelope. These notes, collected and printed closely on the vilest paper, made up the examination questions.

Our form read two authors a term, one Latin and one Greek. It was the Greek that we feared most. Mellish had a sort of genius for picking out absolutely untranslatable passages, and desiring us (in print) to render the same with full notes. This term the book had been Thucydides, Book II, with regard to which I may echo the words of a certain critic when called upon to give his candid opinion of a friend's first novel, 'I dare not say what I think about that book.'

About a week before the commencement of the examinations, the ordinary night-work used to cease, and we were supposed, during that week, to be steadily going over the old ground and arming ourselves for the approaching struggle. There were, I suppose, people who actually did do this, but for my own part I always used to regard those seven days as a blessed period of rest, set apart specially to enable me to keep abreast of the light fiction of the day. And most of the form, so far as I know, thought the same. It was only on the night before the examination that one began to revise in real earnest. One's methods on that night resolved themselves into sitting in a chair and wondering where to begin. Just as one came to a decision, it was bedtime.

'Bradshaw,' I said, as I reached page 103 without having read a line, 'do you know any likely bits?'

Bradshaw looked up from his book. He was attempting to get a general idea of Thucydides' style by reading Pickwick.

'What?' he said.

I obliged with a repetition of my remark.

'Likely bits? Oh, you mean for the Thucydides. I don't know. Mellish never sets the bits any decent ordinary individual would set. I should take my chance if I were you.'

'What are you going to do?'

'I'm going to read Pickwick. Thicksides doesn't come within a mile of it.'

I thought so too.

'But how about tomorrow?'

'Oh, I shan't be there,' he said, as if it were the most ordinary of statements.

'Not there! Why, have you been sacked?'

This really seemed the only possible explanation. Such an event would not have come as a surprise. It was always a matter for wonder to me why the authorities never sacked Bradshaw, or at the least requested him to leave. Possibly it was another case of the ass and the bundles of hay. They could not make up their minds which special misdemeanour of his to attack first.

'No, I've not been sacked,' said Bradshaw.

A light dawned upon me.

'Oh,' I said, 'you're going to slumber in.' For the benefit of the uninitiated, I may mention that to slumber in is to stay in the House during school on a pretence of illness.

'That,' replied the man of mystery, with considerable asperity, 'is exactly the silly rotten kid's idea that would come naturally to a complete idiot like you.'

As a rule, I resent being called a complete idiot, but this was not the time for asserting one's personal dignity. I had to know what Bradshaw's scheme for evading the examination was. Perhaps there might be room for two in it; in which case I should have been exceedingly glad to have lent my moral support to it. I pressed for an explanation.

'You may jaw,' said Bradshaw at last, 'as much as you jolly

34

well please, but I'm not going to give this away. All you're going to know is that I shan't be there tomorrow.'

'I bet you are, and I bet you do a jolly rank paper too,' I said, remembering that the sceptic is sometimes vouchsafed revelations to which the most devout believer may not aspire. It is, for instance, always the young man who scoffs at ghosts that the family spectre chooses as his audience. But it required more than a mere sneer or an empty gibe to pump information out of Bradshaw. He took me up at once.

'What'll you bet?' he said.

Now I was prepared to wager imaginary sums to any extent he might have cared to name, but as my actual worldly wealth at that moment consisted of one penny, and my expectations were limited to the shilling pocket-money which I should receive on the following Saturday—half of which was already mortgaged—it behoved me to avoid doing anything rash with my ready money. But, since a refusal would have meant the downfall of my arguments, I was obliged to name a figure. I named an even sixpence. After all, I felt, I must win. By what means, other than illness, could Bradshaw possibly avoid putting in an appearance at the Thucydides examination?

'All right,' said Bradshaw, 'an even sixpence. You'll lose.'

'Slumbering in barred.'

'Of course.'

'Real illness barred too,' I said. Bradshaw is a man of resource, and has been known to make himself genuinely ill in similar emergencies.

'Right you are. Slumbering in and real illness both barred. Anything else you'd like to bar?'

I thought.

'No. Unless—' an idea struck me—'You're not going to run away?'

Bradshaw scorned to answer the question.

'Now you'd better buck up with your work,' he said, opening his book again. 'You've got about as long odds as anyone ever got. But you'll lose all the same.'

It scarcely seemed possible. And yet—Bradshaw was generally right. If he said he had a scheme for doing—though it was generally for not doing—something, it rarely failed to come off. I thought of my sixpence, my only sixpence, and felt a distinct pang of remorse. After all, only the other day the chaplain had said how wrong it was to bet. By Jove, so he had. Decent man the chaplain. Pity to do anything he would disapprove of. I was on the point of recalling my wager, when before my mind's eye rose a vision of Bradshaw rampant and sneering, and myself writhing in my chair a crushed and scored-off wreck. I drew the line at that. I valued my self-respect at more than sixpence. If it had been a shilling now—. So I set my teeth and turned once more to my Thucydides. Bradshaw, having picked up the thread of his story again, emitted hoarse chuckles like minute guns, until I very nearly rose and fell upon him. It is maddening to listen to a person laughing and not to know the joke.

'You will be allowed two hours for this paper,' said Mellish on the following afternoon, as he returned to his desk after distributing the Thucydides questions. 'At five minutes to four I shall begin to collect your papers, but those who wish may go on till ten past. Write only on one side of the paper, and put your names in the top right-hand corner. Marks will be given for neatness. Any boy whom I see looking at his neighbour's—where's Bradshaw?'

It was already five minutes past the hour. The latest of the late always had the decency to appear at least by three minutes past.

'Has anybody seen Bradshaw?' repeated Mellish. 'You, what's-your-name—' (I am what's-your-name, very much at your service) '—you are in his House. Have you seen him?'

I could have pointed out with some pleasure at this juncture that if Cain expressed indignation at being asked where his brother was, I, by a simple sum in proportion, might with even greater justice feel annoyed at having to locate a person who was no relative of mine at all. Did Mr. Mellish expect me to keep an eye on every member of my House? Did Mr. Mellish—in short, what did he mean by it?

This was what I thought. I said, 'No, sir.'

'This is extraordinary,' said Mellish, 'most extraordinary. Why, the boy was in school this morning.'

This was true. The boy had been in school that morning to some purpose, having beaten all records (his own records) in the gentle sport of Mellish-baiting. This evidently occurred to Mellish at the time, for he dropped the subject at once, and told us to begin our papers.

Now I have remarked already that I dare not say what I think of Thucydides, Book II. How then shall I frame my opinion of that examination paper? It was Thucydides, Book II, with the few easy parts left out. It was Thucydides, Book II, with special home-made difficulties added. It was—well, in its way it was a masterpiece. Without going into details—I dislike sensational and realistic writing—I may say that I personally was not one of those who required an extra ten minutes to finish their papers. I finished mine at half-past two, and amused myself for the remaining hour and a half by writing neatly on several sheets of foolscap exactly what I thought of Mr. Mellish, and precisely what I hoped would happen to him some day. It was grateful and comforting.

At intervals I wondered what had become of Bradshaw. I was not surprised at his absence. At first I had feared that he would keep his word in that matter. As time went on I knew that he would. At more frequent intervals I wondered how I should enjoy being a bankrupt.

Four o'clock came round, and found me so engrossed in putting the finishing touches to my excursus of Mr. Mellish's character, that I stayed on in the form-room till ten past. Two other members of the form stayed too, writing with the despairing energy of those who had five minutes to say what they would like to spread over five hours. At last Mellish collected the papers. He seemed a trifle surprised when I gave up my modest three sheets. Brown and Morrison, who had their eye on the form prize, each gave up reams. Brown told me subsequently that he had only had time to do sixteen sheets, and wanted to know whether I had adopted Rutherford's emendation in preference to the old reading in Question II. My prolonged stay had made him regard me as a possible rival.

I dwell upon this part of my story, because it has an important bearing on subsequent events. If I had not waited in the form-room I should not have gone downstairs just behind Mellish. And if I had not gone downstairs just behind Mellish, I should not have been in at the death, that is to say the discovery of Bradshaw, and this story would have been all beginning and middle, and no ending, for I am certain that Bradshaw would never have told me a word. He was a most secretive animal.

I went downstairs, as I say, just behind Mellish. St Austin's, you must know, is composed of three blocks of buildings, the senior, the middle, and the junior, joined by cloisters. We left the senior block by the door. To the captious critic this information may seem superfluous, but let me tell him that I have left the block in my time, and entered it, too, though never, it is true, in the company of a master, in other ways. There are windows.

Our procession of two, Mellish leading by a couple of yards, passed through the cloisters, and came to the middle block, where the Masters' Common Room is. I had no particular reason for going to that block, but it was all on my way to the House, and I knew that Mellish hated having his footsteps dogged. That Thucydides paper rankled slightly.

In the middle block, at the top of the building, far from the haunts of men, is the Science Museum, containing—so I have heard, I have never been near the place myself—two stuffed rats, a case of

37

mouldering butterflies, and other objects of acute interest. The room has a staircase all to itself, and this was the reason why, directly I heard shouts proceeding from that staircase, I deduced that they came from the Museum. I am like Sherlock Holmes, I don't mind explaining my methods.

'Help!' shouted the voice. 'Help!'

The voice was Bradshaw's.

Mellish was talking to M. Gerard, the French master, at the moment. He had evidently been telling him of Bradshaw's non-appearance, for at the sound of his voice they both spun round, and stood looking at the staircase like a couple of pointers.

'Help,' cried the voice again.

Mellish and Gerard bounded up the stairs. I had never seen a French master run before. It was a pleasant sight. I followed. As we reached the door of the Museum, which was shut, renewed shouts filtered through it. Mellish gave tongue.

'Bradshaw!'

'Yes, sir,' from within.

'Are you there?' This I thought, and still think, quite a superfluous question.

'Yes, sir,' said Bradshaw.

'What are you doing in there, Bradshaw? Why were you not in school this afternoon? Come out at once.' This in deep and thrilling tones.

'Please, sir,' said Bradshaw complainingly, 'I can't open the door.' Now, the immediate effect of telling a person that you are unable to open a door is to make him try his hand at it. Someone observes that there are three things which everyone thinks he can do better than anyone else, namely poking a fire, writing a novel, and opening a door.

Gerard was no exception to the rule.

'Can't open the door?' he said. 'Nonsense, nonsense.' And, swooping at the handle, he grasped it firmly, and turned it.

At this point he made an attempt, a very spirited attempt, to lower the world's record for the standing high jump. I have spoken above of the pleasure it gave me to see a French master run. But for good, square enjoyment, warranted free from all injurious chemicals, give me a French master jumping.

'My dear Gerard,' said the amazed Mellish.

'I have received a shock. Dear me, I have received a most terrible shock.'

So had I, only of another kind. I really thought I should have expired in my tracks with the effort of keeping my enjoyment strictly to myself. I saw what had happened. The Museum is lit by electric light. To turn it on one has to shoot the bolt of the door, which, like the handle, is made of metal. It is on the killing two birds with one stone principle. You lock yourself in and light yourself up with one movement. It was plain that the current had gone wrong somehow, run amock, as it were. Mellish meanwhile, instead of being warned by Gerard's fate, had followed his example, and tried to turn the handle. His jump, though quite a creditable effort, fell short of Gerard's by some six inches. I began to feel as if some sort of round game were going on. I hoped that they would not want me to take a hand. I also hoped that the thing would continue for a good while longer. The success of the piece certainly warranted the prolongation of its run. But here I was disappointed. The disturbance had attracted another spectator, Blaize, the science and chemistry master. The matter was hastily explained to him in all its bearings. There was Bradshaw entombed within the Museum, with every prospect of death by starvation, unless he could support life for the next few years on the two stuffed rats and the case of butterflies. The authorities did not see their way to adding a human specimen (youth's size) to the treasures in the Museum, so—how was he to be got out?

The scientific mind is equal to every emergency.

'Bradshaw,' shouted Blaize through the keyhole.

'Sir?'

'Are you there?'

I should imagine that Bradshaw was growing tired of this question by this time. Besides, it cast aspersions on the veracity of Gerard and Mellish. Bradshaw, with perfect politeness, hastened to inform the gentleman that he was there.

'Have you a piece of paper?'

'Will an envelope do, sir?'

'Bless the boy, anything will do so long as it is paper.'

Dear me, I thought, is it as bad as all that? Is Blaize, in despair of ever rescuing the unfortunate prisoner, going to ask him to draw up a 'last dying words' document, to be pushed under the door and despatched to his sorrowing guardian?

'Put it over your hand, and then shoot back the bolt.'

'But, sir, the electricity.'

'Pooh, boy!'

The scientific mind is always intolerant of lay ignorance.

'Pooh, boy, paper is a non-conductor. You won't get hurt.'

Bradshaw apparently acted on his instructions. From the other side of the door came the sharp sound of the bolt as it was shot back, and at the same time the light ceased to shine through the keyhole. A moment later the handle turned, and Bradshaw stepped forth—free!

'Dear me,' said Mellish. 'Now I never knew that before, Blaize. Remarkable. But this ought to be seen to. In the meantime, I had better ask the Headmaster to give out that the Museum is closed until further notice, I think.'

And closed the Museum has been ever since. That further notice has never been given. And yet nobody seems to feel as if an essential part of their life had ceased to be, so to speak. Curious. Bradshaw, after a short explanation, was allowed to go away without a stain—that is to say, without any additional stain—on his character. We left the authorities discussing the matter, and went downstairs.

'Sixpence isn't enough,' I said, 'take this penny. It's all I've got. You shall have the sixpence on Saturday.'

'Thanks,' said Bradshaw.' Was the Thucydides paper pretty warm?'

'Warmish. But, I say, didn't you get a beastly shock when you locked the door?'

'I did the week before last, the first time I ever went to the place. This time I was more or less prepared for it. Blaize seems to think that paper dodge a special invention of his own. He'll be taking out a patent for it one of these days. Why, every kid knows that paper doesn't conduct electricity.'

'I didn't,' I said honestly.

'You don't know much,' said Bradshaw, with equal honesty.

'I don't,' I replied. 'Bradshaw, you're a great man, but you missed the best part of it all.'

'What, the Thucydides paper?' asked he with a grin.

'No, you missed seeing Gerard jump quite six feet.'

Bradshaw's face expressed keen disappointment.

'No, did he really? Oh, I say, I wish I'd seen it.'

The moral of which is that the wicked do not always prosper. If Bradshaw had not been in the Museum, he might have seen Gerard jump six feet, which would have made him happy for weeks. On second thoughts, though, that does not work out quite right, for if Bradshaw had not been in the Museum, Gerard would not have jumped at all. No, better put it this way. I was virtuous, and I had the pleasure of witnessing the sight I have referred to. But then there was the Thucydides paper, which Bradshaw missed but which I did not. No. On consideration, the moral of this story shall be withdrawn and submitted to a committee of experts. Perhaps they will be able to say what it is.

7

THE BABE AND THE DRAGON

The annual inter-house football cup at St Austin's lay between Dacre's, who were the holders, and Merevale's, who had been runner-up in the previous year, and had won it altogether three times out of the last five. The cup was something of a tradition in Merevale's, but of late Dacre's had become serious rivals, and, as has been said before, were the present holders.

This year there was not much to choose between the two teams. Dacre's had three of the First Fifteen and two of the Second; Merevale's two of the First and four of the Second. St Austin's being not altogether a boarding-school, many of the brightest stars of the teams were day boys, and there was, of course, always the chance that one of these would suddenly see the folly of his ways, reform, and become a member of a House.

This frequently happened, and this year it was almost certain to happen again, for no less a celebrity than MacArthur, commonly known as the Babe, had been heard to state that he was negotiating with his parents to that end. Which House he would go to was at present uncertain. He did not know himself, but it would, he said, probably be one of the two favourites for the cup. This lent an added interest to the competition, for the presence of the Babe would almost certainly turn the scale. The Babe's nationality was Scots, and, like most Scotsmen, he could play football more than a little. He was the safest, coolest centre three-quarter the School had, or had had for some time. He shone in all branches of the game, but especially in tackling. To see the Babe spring apparently from nowhere, in the middle of an inter-school match, and bring down with violence a man who had passed the back, was an intellectual treat. Both Dacre's and Merevale's, therefore, yearned for his advent exceedingly. The reasons which finally decided his choice were rather curious. They arose in the following manner:

The Babe's sister was at Girton. A certain Miss Florence Beezley was also at Girton. When the Babe's sister revisited the ancestral home at the end of the term, she brought Miss Beezley with her to spend a week. What she saw in Miss Beezley was to the Babe a matter for wonder, but she must have liked her, or she would not have gone out of her way to seek her company. Be that as it may, the Babe would have gone a very long way out of his way to avoid her company. He led a fine, healthy, out-of-doors life during that week, and doubtless did himself a lot of good. But times will occur when it is imperative that a man shall be under the family roof. Meal-times, for instance. The Babe could not subsist without food, and he was obliged, Miss Beezley or no Miss Beezley, to present himself on these occasions. This, by the way, was in the Easter holidays, so that there was no school to give him an excuse for absence.

Breakfast was a nightmare, lunch was rather worse, and as for dinner, it was quite unspeakable. Miss Beezley seemed to gather force during the day. It was not the actual presence of the lady that revolted the Babe, for that was passable enough. It was her conversation that killed. She refused to let the Babe alone. She was intensely learned herself, and seemed to take a morbid delight in dissecting his ignorance, and showing everybody the pieces. Also, she persisted in calling him Mr. MacArthur in a way that seemed somehow to point out and emphasize his youthfulness. She added it to her remarks as a sort of after-thought or echo.

'Do you read Browning, Mr. MacArthur?' she would say suddenly, having apparently waited carefully until she saw that his mouth was full.

The Babe would swallow convulsively, choke, blush, and finally say—

'No, not much.'

'Ah!' This in a tone of pity not untinged with scorn.

'When you say "not much", Mr. MacArthur, what exactly do you mean? Have you read any of his poems?'

'Oh, yes, one or two.'

'Ah! Have you read "Pippa Passes"?'

'No, I think not.'

'Surely you must know, Mr. MacArthur, whether you have or not. Have you read "Fifine at the Fair"?'

'No.'

'Have you read "Sordello"?'

'No.'

'What have you read, Mr. MacArthur?'

Brought to bay in this fashion, he would have to admit that he had read 'The Pied Piper of Hamelin', and not a syllable more, and Miss Beezley would look at him for a moment and sigh softly. The Babe's subsequent share in the conversation, provided the Dragon made no further onslaught, was not large.

One never-to-be-forgotten day, shortly before the end of her

42

visit, a series of horrible accidents resulted in their being left to lunch together alone. The Babe had received no previous warning, and when he was suddenly confronted with this terrible state of affairs he almost swooned. The lady's steady and critical inspection of his style of carving a chicken completed his downfall. His previous experience of carving had been limited to those entertainments which went by the name of 'study-gorges', where, if you wanted to help a chicken, you took hold of one leg, invited an accomplice to attach himself to the other, and pulled.

But, though unskilful, he was plucky and energetic. He lofted the bird out of the dish on to the tablecloth twice in the first minute. Stifling a mad inclination to call out 'Fore!' or something to that effect, he laughed a hollow, mirthless laugh, and replaced the errant fowl. When a third attack ended in the same way, Miss Beezley asked permission to try what she could do. She tried, and in two minutes the chicken was neatly dismembered. The Babe re-seated himself in an over-wrought state.

'Tell me about St Austin's, Mr. MacArthur,' said Miss Beezley, as the Babe was trying to think of something to say—not about the weather. 'Do you play football?'

'Yes.'

'Ah!'

A prolonged silence.

'Do you—' began the Babe at last.

'Tell me—' began Miss Beezley, simultaneously.

'I beg your pardon,' said the Babe; 'you were saying—?'

'Not at all, Mr. MacArthur. You were saying—?'

'I was only going to ask you if you played croquet?'

'Yes; do you?'

'No.'

'Ah!'

'If this is going to continue,' thought the Babe, 'I shall be reluctantly compelled to commit suicide.'

There was another long pause.

'Tell me the names of some of the masters at St Austin's, Mr. MacArthur,' said Miss Beezley. She habitually spoke as if she were an examination paper, and her manner might have seemed to some to verge upon the autocratic, but the Babe was too thankful that the question was not on Browning or the higher algebra to notice this. He reeled off a list of names.

'... Then there's Merevale—rather a decent sort—and Dacre.'

'What sort of a man is Mr. Dacre?'

'Rather a rotter, I think.'

43

'What is a rotter, Mr. MacArthur?'

'Well, I don't know how to describe it exactly. He doesn't play cricket or anything. He's generally considered rather a crock.'

'Really! This is very interesting, Mr. MacArthur. And what is a crock? I suppose what it comes to,' she added, as the Babe did his best to find a definition, 'is this, that you yourself dislike him.' The Babe admitted the impeachment. Mr. Dacre had a finished gift of sarcasm which had made him writhe on several occasions, and sarcastic masters are rarely very popular.

'Ah!' said Miss Beezley. She made frequent use of that monosyllable. It generally gave the Babe the same sort of feeling as he had been accustomed to experience in the happy days of his childhood when he had been caught stealing jam.

Miss Beezley went at last, and the Babe felt like a convict who has just received a free pardon.

One afternoon in the following term he was playing fives with Charteris, a prefect in Merevale's House. Charteris was remarkable from the fact that he edited and published at his own expense an unofficial and highly personal paper, called The Glow Worm, which was a great deal more in demand than the recognized School magazine, The Austinian, and always paid its expenses handsomely.

Charteris had the journalistic taint very badly. He was always the first to get wind of any piece of School news. On this occasion he was in possession of an exclusive item. The Babe was the first person to whom he communicated it.

'Have you heard the latest romance in high life, Babe?' he observed, as they were leaving the court. 'But of course you haven't. You never do hear anything.'

'Well?' asked the Babe, patiently.

'You know Dacre?'

'I seem to have heard the name somewhere.'

'He's going to be married.'

'Yes. Don't trouble to try and look interested. You're one of those offensive people who mind their own business and nobody else's. Only I thought I'd tell you. Then you'll have a remote chance of understanding my quips on the subject in next week's Glow Worm. You laddies frae the north have to be carefully prepared for the subtler flights of wit.'

'Thanks,' said the Babe, placidly. 'Good-night.'

The Headmaster intercepted the Babe a few days after he was going home after a scratch game of football. 'MacArthur,' said he, 'you pass Mr. Dacre's House, do you not, on your way home? Then would you mind asking him from me to take preparation tonight? I find I shall be unable to be there.' It was the custom at St Austin's for the Head to preside at preparation once a week; but he performed this duty, like the celebrated Irishman, as often as he could avoid it.

The Babe accepted the commission. He was shown into the drawing-room. To his consternation, for he was not a society man, there appeared to be a species of tea-party going on. As the door opened, somebody was just finishing a remark.

'... faculty which he displayed in such poems as "Sordello",' said the voice.

The Babe knew that voice.

He would have fled if he had been able, but the servant was already announcing him. Mr. Dacre began to do the honours.

'Mr. MacArthur and I have met before,' said Miss Beezley, for it was she. 'Curiously enough, the subject which we have just been discussing is one in which he takes, I think, a great interest. I was saying, Mr. MacArthur, when you came in, that few of Tennyson's works show the poetic faculty which Browning displays in "Sordello".'

The Babe looked helplessly at Mr. Dacre.

'I think you are taking MacArthur out of his depth there,' said Mr. Dacre. 'Was there something you wanted to see me about, MacArthur?'

The Babe delivered his message.

'Oh, yes, certainly,' said Mr. Dacre. 'Shall you be passing the School House tonight? If so, you might give the Headmaster my compliments, and say I shall be delighted.'

The Babe had had no intention of going out of his way to that extent, but the chance of escape offered by the suggestion was too good to be missed. He went.

On his way he called at Merevale's, and asked to see Charteris.

'Look here, Charteris,' he said, 'you remember telling me that Dacre was going to be married?'

'Yes.'

'Well, do you know her name by any chance?'

'I ken it weel, ma braw Hielander. She is a Miss Beezley.'

'Great Scott!' said the Babe.

'Hullo! Why, was your young heart set in that direction? You amaze and pain me, Babe. I think we'd better have a story on the subject in The Glow Worm, with you as hero and Dacre as villain. It shall end happily, of course. I'll write it myself.'

'You'd better,' said the Babe, grimly. 'Oh, I say, Charteris.'

'Well?'

'When I come as a boarder, I shall be a House-prefect, shan't I, as I'm in the Sixth?'

'Yes.'

'And prefects have to go to breakfast and supper, and that sort of thing, pretty often with the House-beak, don't they?'

'Such are the facts of the case.'

'Thanks. That's all. Go away and do some work. Good-night.'

The cup went to Merevale's that year. The Babe played a singularly brilliant game for them.

8

THE MANOEUVRES OF CHARTERIS

Chapter 1

'Might I observe, sir—'
'You may observe whatever you like,' said the referee kindly. 'Twenty-five.'
'The rules say—'
'I have given my decision. Twenty-five!' A spot of red appeared on the official cheek. The referee, who had been heckled since the kick-off, was beginning to be annoyed.
'The ball went behind without bouncing, and the rules say—'
'Twenty-FIVE!!' shouted the referee. 'I am perfectly well aware what the rules say.' And he blew his whistle with an air of finality. The secretary of the Bargees' F.C. subsided reluctantly, and the game was restarted.

The Bargees' match was a curious institution. Their real name was the Old Crockfordians. When, a few years before, the St Austin's secretary had received a challenge from them, dated from Stapleton, where their secretary happened to reside, he had argued within himself as follows: 'This sounds all right. Old Crockfordians? Never heard of Crockford. Probably some large private school somewhere. Anyhow, they're certain to be decent fellows.' And he arranged the fixture. It then transpired that Old Crockford was a village, and, from the appearance of the team on the day of battle, the Old Crockfordians seemed to be composed exclusively of the riff-raff of same. They wore green shirts with a bright yellow leopard over the heart, and C.F.C. woven in large letters about the chest. One or two of the outsides played in caps, and the team to a man criticized the referee's decisions with point and pungency. Unluckily, the first year saw a weak team of Austinians rather badly beaten, with the result that it became a point of honour to wipe this off the slate before the fixture could be cut out of the card. The next year was also unlucky. The Bargees managed to score a penalty goal in the first half, and won on that. The match resulted in a draw in the following season, and by this time the thing had become an annual event.

Now, however, the School was getting some of its own back. The Bargees had brought down a player of some reputation from the North, and were as strong as ever in the scrum. But St Austin's had a great team, and were carrying all before them. Charteris and Graham at half had the ball out to their centres in a way which made Merevale, who looked after the football of the School, feel that life was worth living. And when once it was out, things happened rapidly. MacArthur, the captain of the team, with Thomson as his fellow-centre, and Welch and Bannister on the wings, did what they liked with the Bargees' three-quarters. All the School outsides had scored, even the back, who dropped a neat goal. The player from the North had scarcely touched the ball during the whole game, and altogether the Bargees were becoming restless and excited.

The kick-off from the twenty-five line which followed upon the small discussion alluded to above, reached Graham. Under ordinary circumstances he would have kicked, but in a winning game original methods often pay. He dodged a furious sportsman in green and yellow, and went away down the touch-line. He was almost through when he stumbled. He recovered himself, but too late. Before he could pass, someone was on him. Graham was not heavy, and his opponent was muscular. He was swung off his feet, and the next moment the two came down together, Graham underneath. A sharp pain shot through his shoulder.

A doctor emerged from the crowd—there is always a doctor in a crowd—and made an examination.

'Anything bad?' asked the referee.

'Collar-bone,' said the doctor. 'The usual, you know. Rather badly smashed. Nothing dangerous, of course. Be all right in a month or so. Stop his playing. Rather a pity. Much longer before half-time?'

'No. I was just going to blow the whistle when this happened.'

The injured warrior was carried off, and the referee blew his whistle for half-time.

'I say, Charteris,' said MacArthur, 'who the deuce am I to put half instead of Graham?'

'Rogers used to play half in his childhood, I believe. But, I say, did you ever see such a scrag? Can't you protest, or something?'

'My dear chap, how can I? It's on our own ground. These Bargee beasts are visitors, if you come to think of it. I'd like to wring the chap's neck who did it. I didn't spot who it was. Did you see?'

'Rather. Their secretary. That man with the beard. I'll get Prescott to mark him this half.'

Prescott was the hardest tackler in the School. He accepted

the commission cheerfully, and promised to do his best by the bearded one.

Charteris certainly gave him every opportunity. When he threw the ball out of touch, he threw it neatly to the criminal with the beard, and Prescott, who stuck to him closer than a brother, had generally tackled him before he knew what had happened. After a time he began to grow thoughtful, and when there was a line-out went and stood among the three-quarters. In this way much of Charteris's righteous retribution miscarried, but once or twice he had the pleasure and privilege of putting in a piece of tackling on his own account. The match ended with the enemy still intact, but considerably shaken. He was also rather annoyed. He spoke to Charteris on the subject as they were leaving the field.

'I was watching you,' he said, apropos of nothing apparently.

'That must have been nice for you,' said Charteris.

'You wait.'

'Certainly. Any time you're passing, I'm sure—'

'You ain't 'eard the last of me yet.'

'That's something of a blow,' said Charteris cheerfully, and they parted.

Charteris, having got into his blazer, ran after Welch and MacArthur, and walked back with them to the House. All three of them were at Merevale's.

'Poor old Tony,' said MacArthur. 'Where have they taken him to? The House?'

'Yes,' said Welch. 'I say, Babe, you ought to scratch this match next year. Tell 'em the card's full up or something.'

'Oh, I don't know. One expects fairly rough play in this sort of game. After all, we tackle pretty hard ourselves. I know I always try and go my hardest. If the man happens to be brittle, that's his lookout,' concluded the bloodthirsty Babe.

'My dear man,' said Charteris, 'there's all the difference between a decent tackle and a bally scrag like the one that doubled Tony up. You can't break a chap's collar-bone without trying to.'

'Well, if you come to think of it, I suppose the man must have been fairly riled. You can't expect a man to be in an angelic temper when his side's been licked by thirty points.'

The Babe was one of those thoroughly excellent persons who always try, when possible, to make allowances for everybody.

'Well, dash it,' said Charteris indignantly, 'if he had lost his hair he might have drawn the line at falling on Tony like that. It wasn't the tackling part of it that crocked him. The beast simply jumped on him like a Hooligan. Anyhow, I made him sit up a bit before we finished. I gave Prescott the tip to mark him out of touch. Have you ever been collared by Prescott? It's a liberal education. Now, there you are, you see. Take Prescott. He's never crocked a man seriously in his life. I don't count being winded. That's absolutely an accident. Well, there you are, then. Prescott weighs thirteen-ten, and he's all muscle, and he goes like a battering-ram. You'll own that. He goes as hard as he jolly well knows how, and yet the worst he has ever done is to lay a man out for a couple of minutes while he gets his wind back. Well, compare him with this Bargee man. The Bargee weighs a stone less and isn't nearly as strong, and yet he smashes Tony's collar-bone. It's all very well, Babe, but you can't get away from it. Prescott tackles fairly and the Bargee scrags.'

'Yes,' said MacArthur, 'I suppose you're right.'

'Rather,' said Charteris. 'I wish I'd broken his neck.'

'By the way,' said Welch, 'you were talking to him after the match. What was he saying?'

Charteris laughed.

'By Jove, I'd forgotten; he said I hadn't heard the last of him, and that I was to wait.'

'What did you say?'

'Oh, I behaved beautifully. I asked him to be sure and look in any time he was passing, and after a few chatty remarks we parted.'

'I wonder if he meant anything.'

'I believe he means to waylay me with a buckled belt. I shan't stir out except with the Old Man or some other competent bodyguard. "'Orrible outrage, shocking death of a St Austin's schoolboy." It would look rather well on the posters.'

Welch stuck strenuously to the point.

'No, but, look here, Charteris,' he said seriously, 'I'm not rotting. You see, the man lives in Stapleton, and if he knows anything of School rules—'

'Which he doesn't probably. Why should he? Well?'—'If he knows anything of the rules, he'll know that Stapleton's out of bounds, and he may book you there and run you in to Merevale.'

'Yes,' said MacArthur. 'I tell you what, you'd do well to knock off a few of your expeditions to Stapleton. You know you wouldn't go there once a month if it wasn't out of bounds. You'll be a prefect next term. I should wait till then, if I were you.'

'My dear chap, what does it matter? The worst that can happen to you for breaking bounds is a couple of hundred lines, and I've got a capital of four hundred already in stock. Besides, things would be so slow if you always kept in bounds. I always feel like a

50

cross between Dick Turpin and Machiavelli when I go to Stapleton. It's an awfully jolly feeling. Like warm treacle running down your back. It's cheap at two hundred lines.'

'You're an awful fool,' said Welch, rudely but correctly.

Welch was a youth who treated the affairs of other people rather too seriously. He worried over them. This is not a particularly common trait in the character of either boy or man, but Welch had it highly developed. He could not probably have explained exactly why he was worried, but he undoubtedly was. Welch had a very grave and serious mind. He shared a study with Charteris—for Charteris, though not yet a School-prefect, was part owner of a study—and close observation had convinced him that the latter was not responsible for his actions, and that he wanted somebody to look after him. He had therefore elected himself to the post of a species of modified and unofficial guardian angel to him. The duties were heavy, and the remuneration exceedingly light.

'Really, you know,' said MacArthur, 'I don't see what the point of all your lunacy is. I don't know if you're aware of it, but the Old Man's getting jolly sick with you.'

'I didn't know,' said Charteris, 'but I'm very glad to hear it. For hist! I have a ger-rudge against the person. Beneath my ban that mystic man shall suffer, coute que coute, Matilda. He sat upon me—publicly, and the resultant blot on my scutcheon can only be wiped out with blood, or broken rules,' he added.

This was true. To listen to Charteris on the subject, one might have thought that he considered the matter rather amusing than otherwise. This, however, was simply due to the fact that he treated everything flippantly in conversation. But, like the parrot, he thought the more. The actual casus belli had been trivial. At least the mere spectator would have considered it trivial. It had happened after this fashion. Charteris was a member of the School corps. The orderly-room of the School corps was in the junior part of the School buildings. Charteris had been to replace his rifle in that shrine of Mars after a mid-day drill, and on coming out into the passage had found himself in the middle of a junior school 'rag' of the conventional type. Somebody's cap had fallen off, and two hastily picked teams were playing football with it (Association rules). Now, Charteris was not a prefect (that, it may be observed in passing, was another source of bitterness in him towards the Powers, for he was fairly high up in the Sixth, and others of his set, Welch, Thomson, and Tony Graham, who were also in the Sixth—the two last below him in form order—had already received their prefects' caps). Not being a prefect, it would have been officious in him to have stopped the game. So he was passing on with what Mr. Hurry Bungsho Jabberjee, B.A., would have termed a beaming simper of indescribable suavity, when a member of one of the opposing teams, in effecting a G. O. Smithian dribble, cannoned into him. To preserve his balance—this will probably seem a very thin line of defence, but 'I state but the facts'—he grabbed at the disciple of Smith amidst applause, and at that precise moment a new actor appeared on the scene—the Headmaster. Now, of all the things that lay in his province, the Headmaster most disliked to see a senior 'ragging' with a junior. He had a great idea of the dignity of the senior school, and did all that in him lay to see that it was kept up. The greater number of the juniors with whom the senior was found ragging, the more heinous the offence. Circumstantial evidence was dead against Charteris. To all outward appearances he was one of the players in the impromptu football match. The soft and fascinating beams of the simper, to quote Mr. Jabberjee once more, had not yet faded from the act. A well-chosen word or two from the Headmagisterial lips put a premature end to the football match, and Charteris was proceeding on his way when the Headmaster called him. He stopped. The Headmaster was angry. So angry, indeed, that he did what in a more lucid interval he would not have done. He hauled a senior over the coals in the hearing of a number of juniors, one of whom (unidentified) giggled loudly. As Charteris had on previous occasions observed, the Old Man, when he did start to take a person's measure, didn't leave out much. The address was not long, but it covered a great deal of ground. The section of it which chiefly rankled in Charteris's mind, and which had continued to rankle ever since, was that in which the use of the word 'buffoon' had occurred. Everybody who has a gift of humour and (very naturally) enjoys exercising it, hates to be called a buffoon. It was Charteris's one weak spot. Every other abusive epithet in the language slid off him without penetrating or causing him the least discomfort. The word 'buffoon' went home, right up to the hilt. And, to borrow from Mr. Jabberjee for positively the very last time, he had observed (mentally): 'Henceforward I will perpetrate heaps of the lowest dregs of vice.' He had, in fact, started a perfect bout of breaking rules, simply because they were rules. The injustice of the thing rankled. No one so dislikes being punished unjustly as the person who might have been punished justly on scores of previous occasions, if he had only been found out. To a certain extent, Charteris ran amok. He broke bounds and did little work, and—he was beginning gradually to find this out—got thoroughly tired of it all. Offended dignity, however, still kept him at it, and much as he would have preferred to have resumed a less feverish type of existence, he did not do so.

'I have a ger-rudge against the man,' he said.

'You are an idiot, really,' said Welch.

'Welch,' said Charteris, by way of explanation to MacArthur, 'is a lad of coarse fibre. He doesn't understand the finer feelings. He can't see that I am doing this simply for the Old Man's good. Spare the rod, spile the choild. Let's go and have a look at Tony when we're changed. He'll be in the sick-room if he's anywhere.'

'All right,' said the Babe, as he went into his study. 'Buck up. I'll toss you for first bath in a second.'

Charteris walked on with Welch to their sanctum.

'You know,' said Welch seriously, stooping to unlace his boots, 'rotting apart, you really are a most awful ass. I wish I could get you to see it.'

'Never you mind, ducky,' said Charteris, 'I'm all right. I'll look after myself.'

Chapter 2

It was about a week after the Bargees' match that the rules respecting bounds were made stricter, much to the popular indignation. The penalty for visiting Stapleton without leave was increased from two hundred lines to two extra lessons. The venomous characteristic of extra lesson was that it cut into one's football, for the criminal was turned into a form-room from two till four on half-holidays, and so had to scratch all athletic engagements for the day, unless he chose to go for a solitary run afterwards. In the cricket term the effect of this was not so deadly. It was just possible that you might get an innings somewhere after four o'clock, even if only at the nets. But during the football season—it was now February—to be in extra lesson meant a total loss of everything that makes life endurable, and the School protested (to one another, in the privacy of their studies) with no uncertain voice against this barbarous innovation.

The reason for the change had been simple. At the corner of the High Street at Stapleton was a tobacconist's shop, and Mr. Prater, strolling in one evening to renew his stock of Pioneer, was interested to observe P. St H. Harrison, of Merevale's, purchasing a consignment of 'Girl of my Heart' cigarettes (at twopence-halfpenny the packet of twenty, including a coloured picture of Lord Kitchener). Now, Mr. Prater was one of the most sportsmanlike of masters. If he had merely met Harrison out of bounds, and it had been possible to have overlooked him, he would have done so. But such a proceeding in the interior of a small shop was impossible. There was nothing to palliate the crime. The tobacconist also kept the wolf from the door, and lured the juvenile population of the neighbourhood to it, by selling various weird brands of sweets, but it was only too obvious that Harrison was not after these. Guilt was in his eye, and the packet of cigarettes in his hand. Also Harrison's House cap was fixed firmly at the back of his head. Mr. Prater finished buying his Pioneer, and went out without a word. That night it was announced to Harrison that the Headmaster wished to see him. The Headmaster saw him, though for a certain period of the interview he did not see the Headmaster, having turned his back on him by request. On the following day Stapleton was placed doubly out of bounds.

Tony, who was still in bed, had not heard the news when Charteris came to see him on the evening of the day on which the edict had gone forth.

'How are you getting on?' asked Charteris.

'Oh, fairly well. It's rather slow.'

'The grub seems all right.' Charteris absently reached out for a slice of cake.

'Not bad.'

'And you don't have to do any work.'

'No.'

'Well, then, it seems to me you're having a jolly good time. What don't you like about it?'

'It's so slow, being alone all day.'

'Makes you appreciate intellectual conversation all the more when you get it. Mine, for instance.'

'I want something to read.'

'I'll bring you a Sidgwick's Greek Prose Composition, if you like. Full of racy stories.'

'I've read 'em, thanks.'

'How about Jebb's Homer? You'd like that. Awfully interesting. Proves that there never was such a man as Homer, you know, and that the Iliad and the Odyssey were produced by evolution. General style, quietly funny. Make you roar.'

'Don't be an idiot. I'm simply starving for something to read. Haven't you got anything?'

'You've read all mine.'

'Hasn't Welch got any books?'

'Not one. He bags mine when he wants to read. I'll tell you what I will do if you like.'

'What?'

'Go into Stapleton, and borrow something from Adamson.' Adamson was the College doctor.

'By Jove, that's not a bad idea.'

'It's a dashed good idea, which wouldn't have occurred to anybody but a genius. I've been quite a pal of Adamson's ever since I had the flu. I go to tea with him occasionally, and we talk medical shop. Have you ever tried talking medical shop during tea? Nothing like it for giving you an appetite.'

'Has he got anything readable?'

'Rather. Have you ever tried anything of James Payn's?'

'I've read Terminations, or something,' said Tony doubtfully, 'but he's so obscure.'

'Don't,' said Charteris sadly, 'please don't. Terminations is by one Henry James, and there is a substantial difference between him and James Payn. Anyhow, if you want a short biography of James Payn, he wrote a hundred books, and they're all simply ripping, and Adamson has got a good many of them, and I'm hoping to borrow a couple—any two will do—and you're going to read them. I know one always bars a book that's recommended to one, but you've got no choice. You're not going to get anything else till you've finished those two.'

'All right,' said Tony. 'But Stapleton's out of bounds. I suppose Merevale'll give you leave to go in.'

'He won't,' said Charteris. 'I shan't ask him. On principle. So long.'

On the following afternoon Charteris went into Stapleton. The distance by road was almost exactly one mile. If you went by the fields it was longer, because you probably lost your way.

Dr Adamson's house was in the High Street. Charteris knocked at the door. The servant was sorry, but the doctor was out. Her tone seemed to suggest that, if she had had any say in the matter, he would have remained in. Would Charteris come in and wait? Charteris rather thought he would. He waited for half an hour, and then, as the absent medico did not appear to be coming, took two books from the shelf, wrote a succinct note explaining what he had done, and why he had done it, hoping the doctor would not mind, and went out with his literary trophies into the High Street again.

The time was now close on five o'clock. Lock-up was not till a quarter past six—six o'clock nominally, but the doors were always left open till a quarter past. It would take him about fifteen minutes to get back, less if he trotted. Obviously, the thing to do here was to spend a thoughtful quarter of an hour or so inspecting the sights of the town. These were ordinarily not numerous, but this particular day happened to be market day, and there was a good deal going on. The High Street was full of farmers, cows, and other animals, the majority of the former well on the road to intoxication. It is, of course, extremely painful to see a man in such a condition, but when such a person is endeavouring to count a perpetually moving drove of pigs, the onlooker's pain is sensibly diminished. Charteris strolled along the High Street observing these and other phenomena with an attentive eye. Opposite the Town Hall he was button-holed by a perfect stranger, whom, by his conversation, he soon recognized as the Stapleton 'character'. There is a 'character' in every small country town. He is not a bad character; still less is he a good character. He is just a 'character' pure and simple. This particular man—or rather, this man, for he was anything but particular—apparently took a great fancy to Charteris at first sight. He backed him gently against a wall, and insisted on telling him an interminable anecdote of his shady past, when, it seemed, he had been a 'super' in some travelling company. The plot of the story, as far as Charteris could follow it, dealt with a theatrical tour in Dublin, where some person or persons unknown had, with malice prepense, scattered several pounds of snuff on the stage previous to a performance of Hamlet; and, according to the 'character', when the ghost of Hamlet's father sneezed steadily throughout his great scene, there was not a dry eye in the house. The 'character' had concluded that anecdote, and was half-way through another, when Charteris, looking at his watch, found that it was almost six o'clock. He interrupted one of the 'character's' periods by diving past him and moving rapidly down the street. The historian did not seem to object. Charteris looked round and saw that he had button-holed a fresh victim. He was still gazing in one direction and walking in another, when he ran into somebody.

'Sorry,' said Charteris hastily. 'Hullo!'

It was the secretary of the Old Crockfordians, and, to judge from the scowl on that gentleman's face, the recognition was mutual.

'It's you, is it?' said the secretary in his polished way.

'I believe so,' said Charteris.

'Out of bounds,' observed the man.

Charteris was surprised. This grasp of technical lore on the part of a total outsider was as unexpected as it was gratifying.

'What do you know about bounds?' said Charteris.

'I know you ain't allowed to come 'ere, and you'll get it 'ot from your master for coming.'

'Ah, but he won't know. I shan't tell him, and I'm sure you will respect my secret.'

Charteris smiled in a winning manner.

'Ho!' said the man, 'Ho indeed!'

There is something very clinching about the word 'Ho'. It seems definitely to apply the closure to any argument. At least, I have never yet met anyone who could tell me the suitable repartee.

'Well,' said Charteris affably, 'don't let me keep you. I must be going on.'

'Ho!' observed the man once more. 'Ho indeed!'

'That's a wonderfully shrewd remark,' said Charteris. 'I can see that, but I wish you'd tell me exactly what it means.'

'You're out of bounds.'

'Your mind seems to run in a groove. You can't get off that bounds business. How do you know Stapleton's out of bounds?'

'I have made enquiries,' said the man darkly.

'By Jove,' said Charteris delightedly, 'this is splendid. You're a regular sleuth-hound. I dare say you've found out my name and House too?'

'I may 'ave,' said the man, 'or I may not 'ave.'

'Well, now you mention it, I suppose one of the two contingencies is probable. Well, I'm awfully glad to have met you. Good-bye. I must be going.'

'You're goin' with me.'

'Arm in arm?'

'I don't want to 'ave to take you.'

'No,' said Charteris, 'I should jolly well advise you not to try. This is my way.'

He walked on till he came to the road that led to St Austin's. The secretary of the Old Crockfordians stalked beside him with determined stride.

'Now,' said Charteris, when they were on the road, 'you mustn't mind if I walk rather fast. I'm in a hurry.'

Charteris's idea of walking rather fast was to dash off down the road at quarter-mile pace. The move took the man by surprise, but, after a moment, he followed with much panting. It was evident that he was not in training. Charteris began to feel that the walk home might be amusing in its way. After they had raced some three hundred yards he slowed down to a walk again. It was at this point that his companion evinced a desire to do the rest of the journey with a hand on the collar of his coat.

'If you touch me,' observed Charteris with a surprising knowledge of legal minutiae, 'it'll be a technical assault, and you'll get run in; and you'll get beans anyway if you try it on.'

The man reconsidered matters, and elected not to try it on.

Half a mile from the College Charteris began to walk rather fast again. He was a good half-miler, and his companion was bad at every distance. After a game struggle he dropped to the rear, and finished a hundred yards behind in considerable straits. Charteris shot in at Merevale's door with five minutes to spare, and went up to his study to worry Welch by telling him about it.

'Welch, you remember the Bargee who scragged Tony? Well, there have been all sorts of fresh developments. He's just been pacing me all the way from Stapleton.'

'Stapleton! Have you been to Stapleton? Did Merevale give you leave?'

'No. I didn't ask him.'

'You are an idiot. And now this Bargee man will go straight to the Old Man and run you in. I wonder you didn't think of that.'

'Curious I didn't.'

'I suppose he saw you come in here?'

'Rather. He couldn't have had a better view if he'd paid for a seat. Half a second; I must just run up with these volumes to Tony.'

When he came back he found Welch more serious than ever.

'I told you so,' said Welch. 'You're to go to the Old Man at once. He's just sent over for you. I say, look here, if it's only lines I don't mind doing some of them, if you like.'

Charteris was quite touched by this sporting offer.

'It's awfully good of you,' he said, 'but it doesn't matter, really. I shall be all right.'

Ten minutes later he returned, beaming.

'Well,' said Welch, 'what's he given you?'

'Only his love, to give to you. It was this way. He first asked me if I wasn't perfectly aware that Stapleton was out of bounds. "Sir," says I, "I've known it from childhood's earliest hour." "Ah," says he to me, "did Mr. Merevale give you leave to go in this afternoon?" "No," says I, "I never consulted the gent you mention."'

'Well?'

'Then he ragged me for ten minutes, and finally told me I must go into extra the next two Saturdays.'

'I thought so.'

'Ah, but mark the sequel. When he had finished, I said that I was sorry I had mistaken the rules, but I had thought that a chap was allowed to go into Stapleton if he got leave from a master. "But

58

you said that Mr. Merevale did not give you leave," said he. "Friend of my youth," I replied courteously, "you are perfectly correct. As always. Mr. Merevale did not give me leave, but," I added suavely, "Mr. Dacre did." And I came away, chanting hymns of triumph in a mellow baritone, and leaving him in a dead faint on the sofa. And the Bargee, who was present during the conflict, swiftly and silently vanished away, his morale considerably shattered. And that, my gentle Welch,' concluded Charteris cheerfully, 'put me one up. So pass the biscuits, and let us rejoice if we never rejoice again.'

Chapter 3

The Easter term was nearing its end. Football, with the exception of the final House-match, which had still to come off, was over, and life was in consequence a trifle less exhilarating than it might have been. In some ways the last few weeks before the Easter holidays are quite pleasant. You can put on running shorts and a blazer and potter about the grounds, feeling strong and athletic, and delude yourself into the notion that you are training for the sports. Ten minutes at the broad jump, five with the weight, a few sprints on the track—it is all very amusing and harmless, but it is apt to become monotonous after a time. And if the weather is at all inclined to be chilly, such an occupation becomes impossible.

Charteris found things particularly dull. He was a fair average runner, but there were others far better at every distance, so that he saw no use in mortifying the flesh with strict training. On the other hand, in view of the fact that the final House-match had yet to be played, and that Merevale's was one of the two teams that were going to play it, it behoved him to keep himself at least moderately fit. The genial muffin and the cheery crumpet were still things to be avoided. He thus found himself in a position where, apparently, the few things which it was possible for him to do were barred, and the net result was that he felt slightly dull.

To make matters worse, all the rest of his set were working full time at their various employments, and had no leisure for amusing him. Welch practised hundred-yard sprints daily, and imagined that it would be quite a treat for Charteris to be allowed to time him. So he gave him the stopwatch, saw him safely to the end of the track, and at a given signal dashed off in the approved American style. By the time he reached the tape, dutifully held by two sporting Merevalian juniors, Charteris's attention had generally been attracted elsewhere. 'What time?' Welch would pant. 'By Jove,' Charteris would observe blandly, 'I forgot to look. About a minute and a quarter, I fancy.' At which Welch, who always had a notion that he had done it in ten and a fifth that time, at any rate, would dissemble his joy, and mildly suggest that somebody else should hold the watch. Then there was Jim Thomson, generally a perfect mine of elevating conversation. He was in for the mile and also the half, and refused to talk about anything except those distances, and the best methods for running them in the minimum of time. Charteris began to feel a blue melancholy stealing over him. The Babe, again. He might have helped to while away the long hours, but unfortunately the Babe had been taken very bad with a notion that he was going to win the 'cross-country run, and when, in addition to this, he was seized with a panic with regard to the prospects of the House team in the final, and began to throw out hints concerning strict training, Charteris regarded him as a person to be avoided. If he fled to the Babe for sympathy now, the Babe would be just as likely as not to suggest that he should come for a ten-mile spin with him, to get him into condition for the final Houser. The very thought of a ten-mile spin made Charteris feel faint. Lastly, there was Tony. But Tony's company was worse than none at all. He went about with his arm in a sling, and declined to be comforted. But for his injury, he would by now have been training hard for the Aldershot Boxing Competition, and the fact that he was now definitely out of it had a very depressing effect upon him. He lounged moodily about the gymnasium, watching Menzies, who was to take his place, sparring with the instructor, and refused consolation. Altogether, Charteris found life a distinct bore.

He was reduced to such straits for amusement, that one Wednesday afternoon, finding himself with nothing else to do, he was working at a burlesque and remarkably scurrilous article on 'The Staff, by one who has suffered', which he was going to insert in The Glow Worm, an unofficial periodical which he had started for the amusement of the School and his own and his contributors' profit. He was just warming to his work, and beginning to enjoy himself, when the door opened without a preliminary knock. Charteris deftly slid a piece of blotting-paper over his MS., for Merevale occasionally entered a study in this manner. And though there was nothing about Merevale himself in the article, it would be better perhaps, thought Charteris, if he did not see it. But it was not Merevale. It was somebody far worse. The Babe.

The Babe was clothed as to his body in football clothes, and as to face, in a look of holy enthusiasm. Charteris knew what that look meant. It meant that the Babe was going to try and drag him out for a run.

'Go away, Babe,' he said, 'I'm busy.'

'Why on earth are you slacking in here on this ripping afternoon?'

'Slacking!' said Charteris. 'I like that. I'm doing berrain work, Babe. I'm writing an article on masters and their customs, which will cause a profound sensation in the Common Room. At least it would, if they ever saw it, but they won't. Or I hope they won't for their sake and mine. So run away, my precious Babe, and don't disturb your uncle when he's busy.'

'Rot,' said the Babe firmly, 'you haven't taken any exercise for a week.'

Charteris replied proudly that he had wound up his watch only last night. The Babe refused to accept the remark as relevant to the matter in hand.

'Look here, Alderman,' he said, sitting down on the table, and gazing sternly at his victim, 'it's all very well, you know, but the final comes on in a few days, and you know you aren't in any too good training.'

'I am,' said Charteris, 'I'm as fit as a prize fighter. Simply full of beans. Feel my ribs.'

The Babe declined the offer.

'No, but I say,' he said plaintively, 'I wish you'd treat it seriously. It's getting jolly serious, really. If Dacre's win that cup again this year, that'll make four years running.'

'Not so,' said Charteris, like the mariner of infinite-resource-and-sagacity; 'not so, but far otherwise. It'll only make three.'

'Well, three's bad enough.'

'True, oh king, three is quite bad enough.'

'Well, then, there you are. Now you see.'

Charteris looked puzzled.

'Would you mind explaining that remark?' he said. 'Slowly.'

But the Babe had got off the table, and was prowling round the room, opening cupboards and boxes.

'What are you playing at?' enquired Charteris.

'Where do you keep your footer things?'

'What do you want with my footer things, if you don't mind my asking?'

'I'm going to help you put them on, and then you're coming for a run.'

'Ah,' said Charteris.

'Yes. Just a gentle spin to keep you in training. Hullo, this looks like them.'

He plunged both hands into a box near the window and flung out a mass of football clothes. It reminded Charteris of a terrier digging at a rabbit-hole.

He protested.

'Don't, Babe. Treat 'em tenderly. You'll be spoiling the crease in those bags if you heave 'em about like that. I'm very particular about how I look on the football field. I was always taught to dress myself like a little gentleman, so to speak. Well, now you've seen them, put 'em away.'

'Put 'em on,' said the Babe firmly.

'You are a beast, Babe. I don't want to go for a run. I'm getting too old for violent exercise.'

'Buck up,' said the Babe. 'We mustn't chuck any chances away. Now that Tony can't play, we shall have to do all we know if we want to win.'

'I don't see what need there is to get nervous about it. Considering we've got three of the First three-quarter line, and the Second Fifteen back, we ought to do pretty well.'

'But look at Dacre's scrum. There's Prescott, to start with. He's worth any two of our men put together. Then they've got Carter, Smith, and Hemming out of the first, and Reeve-Jones out of the second. And their outsides aren't so very bad, if you come to think of it. Bannister's in the first, and the other three-quarters are all good. And they've got both the second halves. You'll have practically to look after both of them now that Tony's crocked. And Baddeley has come on a lot this term.'

'Babe,' said Charteris, 'you have reason. I will turn over a new leaf. I will be good. Give me my things and I'll come for a run. Only please don't let it be anything over twenty miles.'

'Good man,' said the gratified Babe. 'We won't go far, and will take it quite easy.'

'I tell you what,' said Charteris. 'Do you know a place called Worbury? I thought you wouldn't, probably. It's only a sort of hamlet, two cottages, three public-houses, and a duck-pond, and that sort of thing. I only know it because Welch and I ran there once last year. It's in the Badgwick direction, about three miles by road, mostly along the level. I vote we muffle up fairly well, blazers and sweaters and so on, run to Worbury, tea at one of the cottages, and back in time for lock-up. How does that strike you?'

'It sounds all right. How about tea though? Are you certain you can get it?'

'Rather. The Oldest Inhabitant is quite a pal of mine.'

Charteris's circle of acquaintances was a standing wonder to the Babe and other Merevalians. He seemed to know everybody in the county.

When once he was fairly started on any business, physical or mental, Charteris generally shaped well. It was the starting that he found the difficulty. Now that he was actually in motion, he was enjoying himself thoroughly. He wondered why on earth he had been so reluctant to come for this run. The knowledge that there were three miles to go, and that he was equal to them, made him feel a new man. He felt fit. And there is nothing like feeling fit for dispelling boredom. He swung along with the Babe at a steady pace.

'There's the cottage,' he said, as they turned a bend of the road, and Worbury appeared a couple of hundred yards away. 'Let's sprint.' They sprinted, and arrived at the door of the cottage with scarcely a yard between them, much to the admiration of the Oldest Inhabitant, who was smoking a thoughtful pipe in his front garden. Mr.s Oldest Inhabitant came out of the cottage at the sound of voices, and Charteris broached the subject of tea. The menu was sumptuous and varied, and even the Babe, in spite of his devotion to strict training, could scarce forbear to smile happily at the mention of hot cakes.

During the mauvais quart d'heure before the meal, Charteris kept up an animated conversation with the Oldest Inhabitant, the Babe joining in from time to time when he could think of anything to say. Charteris appeared to be quite a friend of the family. He enquired after the Oldest Inhabitant's rheumatics. It was gratifying to find that they were distinctly better. How had Mr.s O. I. been since his last visit? Prarper hearty? Excellent. How was the O. I.'s nevvy?

At the mention of his nevvy the O. I. became discursive. He told his audience everything that had happened in connection with the said nevvy for years back. After which he started to describe what he would probably do in the future. Amongst other things, there were going to be some sports at Rutton today week, and his nevvy was going to try and win the cup for what the Oldest Inhabitant vaguely described as 'a race'. He had won it last year. Yes, prarper good runner, his nevvy. Where was Rutton? the Babe wanted to know. About eight miles out of Stapleton, said Charteris, who was well up in local geography. You got there by train. It was the next station.

Mr. s O. I. came out to say that tea was ready, and, being drawn into the conversation on the subject of the Rutton sports, produced a programme of the same, which her nevvy had sent them. From this it seemed that the nevvy's 'spot' event was the egg and spoon race. An asterisk against his name pointed him out as the last year's winner.

'Hullo,' said Charteris, 'I see there's a strangers' mile. I'm a demon at the mile when I'm roused. I think I shall go in for it.'

He handed the programme back and began his tea.

'You know, Babe,' he said, as they were going back that evening, 'I really think I shall go in for that race. It would be a most awful rag. It's the day before the House-match, so it'll just get me fit.'

'Don't be a fool,' said the Babe. 'There would be a fearful row about it if you were found out. You'd get extras for the rest of your life.'

'Well, the final Houser comes off on a Thursday, so it won't affect that.'

'Yes, but still—'

'I shall think about it,' said Charteris. 'You needn't go telling anyone.'

'If you'll take my advice, you'll drop it.'

'Your suggestion has been noted, and will receive due attention,' said Charteris. 'Put on the pace a bit.'

They lengthened their stride, and conversation came to an abrupt end.

Chapter 4

'I shall go, Babe,' said Charteris on the following night.

The Sixth Form had a slack day before them on the morrow, there being a temporary lull in the form-work which occurred about once a week, when there was no composition of any kind to be done. The Sixth did four compositions a week, two Greek and two Latin, and except for these did not bother themselves very much about overnight preparation. The Latin authors which the form were doing were Livy and Virgil, and when either of these were on the next day's programme, most of the Sixth considered that they were justified in taking a night off. They relied on their ability to translate both authors at sight and without previous acquaintance. The popular notion that Virgil is hard rarely appeals to a member of a public school. There are two ways of translating Virgil, the conscientious and the other. He prefers the other.

On this particular night, therefore, work was 'off'. Merevale was over at the Great Hall, taking preparation, and the Sixth-Form Merevalians had assembled in Charteris's study to talk about things in general. It was after a pause of some moments, that had followed upon a lively discussion of the House's prospects in the forthcoming final, that Charteris had spoken.

'I shall go, Babe,' said he.

'Go where?' asked Tony, from the depths of a deck-chair.

'Babe knows.'

The Babe turned to the company and explained.

'The lunatic's going in for the strangers' mile at some sports at Rutton next week. He'll get booked for a cert. He can't see that. I never saw such a man.'

'Rally round,' said Charteris, 'and reason with me. I'll listen. Tony, what do you think about it?'

Tony expressed his opinion tersely, and Charteris thanked him. Welch, who had been reading, now awoke to the fact that a discussion was in progress, and asked for details. The Babe explained once more, and Welch heartily corroborated Tony's remarks. Charteris thanked him too.

'You aren't really going, are you?' asked Welch.

'Rather,' said Charteris.

'The Old Man won't give you leave.'

'Shan't worry the poor man with such trifles.'

'But it's miles out of bounds. Stapleton station is out of bounds to start with. It's against rules to go in a train, and Rutton's even more out of bounds than Stapleton.'

'And as there are sports there,' said Tony, 'the Old Man is certain to put Rutton specially out of bounds for that day. He always bars a St Austin's chap going to a place when there's anything going on there.'

'I don't care. What have I to do with the Old Man's petty prejudices? Now, let me get at my time-table. Here we are. Now then.'

'Don't be a fool,' said Tony,

'Certainly not. Look here, there's a train starts from Stapleton at three. I can catch that all right. Gets to Rutton at three-twenty. Sports begin at three-fifteen. At least, they are supposed to. Over before five, I should think. At least, my race will be, though I must stop to see the Oldest Inhabitant's nevvy win the egg and spoon canter. But that ought to come on before the strangers' race. Train back at a quarter past five. Arrives at a quarter to six. Lock up six-fifteen. That gives me half an hour to get here from Stapleton. What

65

more do you want? I shall do it easily, and ... the odds against my being booked are about twenty-five to one. At which price if any gent present cares to deposit his money, I am willing to take him. Now I'll treat you to a tune, if you're good.'

He went to the cupboard and produced his gramophone. Charteris's musical instruments had at one time been strictly suppressed by the authorities, and, in consequence, he had laid in a considerable stock of them. At last, when he discovered that there was no rule against the use of musical instruments in the House, Merevale had yielded. The stipulation that Charteris should play only before prep. was rigidly observed, except when Merevale was over at the Hall, and the Sixth had no work. On such occasions Charteris felt justified in breaking through the rule. He had a gramophone, a banjo, a penny whistle, and a mouth organ. The banjo, which he played really well, was the most in request, but the gramophone was also popular.

'Turn on "Whistling Rufus",' observed Thomson.

'Whistling Rufus' was duly turned on, giving way after an encore to 'Bluebells'.

'I always weep when I hear this,' said Tony.

'It is beautiful, isn't it?' said Charteris.

I'll be your sweetheart, if you—will be—mine,
All my life, I'll be your valentine.
Bluebells I've gathered—grrhhrh.

The needle of the gramophone, after the manner of its kind, slipped raspingly over the surface of the wax, and the rest of the ballad was lost.

'That,' said Charteris, 'is how I feel with regard to the Old Man. I'd be his sweetheart, if he'd be mine. But he makes no advances, and the stain on my scutcheon is not yet wiped out. I must say I haven't tried gathering bluebells for him yet, nor have I offered my services as a perpetual valentine, but I've been very kind to him in other ways.'

'Is he still down on you?' asked the Babe.

'He hasn't done much lately. We're in a state of truce at present. Did I tell you how I scored about Stapleton?'

'You've only told us about a hundred times,' said the Babe brutally. 'I tell you what, though, he'll score off you if he finds you going to Rutton.'

'Let's hope he won't.'

'He won't,' said Welch suddenly.

66

'Why?'

'Because you won't go. I'll bet you anything you like that you won't go.'

That settled Charteris. It was the sort of remark that always acted on him like a tonic. He had been intending to go all the time, but it was this speech of Welch's that definitely clinched the matter. One of his mottoes for everyday use was 'Let not thyself be scored off by Welch.'

'That's all right,' he said. 'Of course I shall go. What's the next item you'd like on this machine?'

The day of the sports arrived, and the Babe, meeting Charteris at Merevale's gate, made a last attempt to head him off from his purpose.

'How are you going to take your things?' he asked. 'You can't carry a bag. The first beak you met would ask questions.'

If he had hoped that this would be a crushing argument, he was disappointed.

Charteris patted a bloated coat pocket.

'Bags,' he said laconically. 'Vest,' he added, doing the same to his other pocket. 'Shoes,' he concluded, 'you will observe I am carrying in a handy brown paper parcel, and if anybody wants to know what's in it, I shall tell them it's acid drops. Sure you won't come, too?'

'Quite, thanks.'

'All right. So long then. Be good while I'm gone.'

And he passed on down the road that led to Stapleton.

The Rutton Recreation Ground presented, as the Stapleton Herald justly remarked in its next week's issue, 'a gay and animated appearance'. There was a larger crowd than Charteris had expected. He made his way through them, resisting without difficulty the entreaties of a hoarse gentleman in a check suit to have three to two on 'Enery something for the hundred yards, and came at last to the dressing-tent.

At this point it occurred to him that it would be judicious to find out when his race was to start. It was rather a chilly day, and the less time he spent in the undress uniform of shorts the better. He bought a correct card for twopence, and scanned it. The strangers' mile was down for four-fifty. There was no need to change for an hour yet. He wished the authorities could have managed to date the event earlier.

Four-fifty was running it rather fine. The race would be over by about five to five, and it was a walk of some ten minutes to the station, less if he hurried. That would give him ten minutes for recovering from the effects of the race, and changing back into his ordinary clothes again. It would be quick work. But, having come so far, he was not inclined to go back without running in the race. He would never be able to hold his head up again if he did that. He left the dressing-tent, and started on a tour of the field.

The scene was quite different from anything he had ever witnessed before in the way of sports. The sports at St Austin's were decorous to a degree. These leaned more to the rollickingly convivial. It was like an ordinary race-meeting, except that men were running instead of horses. Rutton was a quiet little place for the majority of the year, but it woke up on this day, and was evidently out to enjoy itself. The Rural Hooligan was a good deal in evidence, and though he was comparatively quiet just at present, the frequency with which he visited the various refreshment stalls that dotted the ground gave promise of livelier times in the future. Charteris felt that the afternoon would not be dull.

The hour soon passed, and Charteris, having first seen the Oldest Inhabitant's nevvy romp home in the egg and spoon event, took himself off to the dressing-tent, and began to get into his running clothes. The bell for his race was just ringing when he left the tent. He trotted over to the starting place.

Apparently there was not a very large 'field'. Two weedy-looking youths of about Charteris's age, dressed in blushing pink, put in an appearance, and a very tall, thin man came up almost immediately afterwards. Charteris had just removed his coat, and was about to get to his place on the line, when another competitor arrived, and, to judge by the applause that greeted his appearance, he was evidently a favourite in the locality. It was with shock that Charteris recognized his old acquaintance, the Bargees' secretary.

He was clad in running clothes of a bright orange and a smile of conscious superiority, and when somebody in the crowd called out 'Go it, Jarge!' he accepted the tribute as his due, and waved a condescending hand in the speaker's direction.

Some moments elapsed before he recognized Charteris, and the latter had time to decide upon his line of action. If he attempted concealment in any way, the man would recognize that on this occasion, at any rate, he had, to use an adequate if unclassical expression, got the bulge, and then there would be trouble. By brazening things out, however, there was just a chance that he might make him imagine that there was more in the matter than met the eye, and that, in some mysterious way, he had actually obtained leave to visit Rutton that day. After all, the man didn't know very much about School rules, and the recollection of the recent fiasco in which he had taken part would make him think twice about playing the amateur policeman again, especially in connection with Charteris.

So he smiled genially, and expressed a hope that the man enjoyed robust health.

The man replied by glaring in a simple and unaffected manner.

'Looked up the Headmaster lately?' asked Charteris.

'What are you doing here?'

'I'm going to run. Hope you don't mind.'

'You're out of bounds.'

'That's what you said before. You'd better enquire a bit before you make rash statements. Otherwise, there's no knowing what may happen. Perhaps Mr. Dacre has given me leave.'

The man said something objurgatory under his breath, but forbore to continue the discussion. He was wondering, as Charteris had expected that he would, whether the latter had really got leave or not. It was a difficult problem.

Whether such a result was due to his mental struggles, or whether it was simply to be attributed to his poor running, is open to question, but the fact remains that the secretary of the Old Crockfordians did not shine in the strangers' mile. He came in last but one, vanquishing the pink sportsman by a foot. Charteris, after a hot finish, was beaten on the tape by one of the weedy youths, who exhibited astounding sprinting powers in the last two hundred yards, overhauling Charteris, who had led all the time, in fine style, and scoring what the Stapleton Herald described as a 'highly popular victory'.

As soon as he had recovered his normal stock of wind—which was not immediately—it was borne in upon Charteris that if he wanted to catch the five-fifteen back to Stapleton, he had better be beginning to change. He went to the dressing-tent, and on examining his watch was horrified to find that he had just ten minutes in which to do everything, and the walk to the station, he reflected, was a long five minutes. He literally hurled himself into his clothes, and, disregarding the Bargee, who had entered the tent and seemed to wish to continue the discussion at the point where they had left off, shot off towards the gate nearest the station. He had exactly four minutes and twenty-five seconds in which to complete the journey, and he had just run a mile.

Chapter 5

Fortunately the road was mainly level. On the other hand, he was hampered by an overcoat. After the first hundred yards he took this off, and carried it in an unwieldy parcel. This, he found, answered admirably. Running became easier. He had worked the stiffness out of his legs by this time, and was going well. Three hundred yards from the station it was anybody's race. The exact position of the other competitor, the train, could not be defined. It was at any rate not yet within earshot, which meant that it still had at least a quarter of a mile to go. Charteris considered that he had earned a rest. He slowed down to a walk, but after proceeding at this pace for a few yards, thought that he heard a distant whistle, and dashed on again. Suddenly a raucous bellow of laughter greeted his ears from a spot in front of him, hidden from his sight by a bend in the road.

'Somebody slightly tight,' thought Charteris, rapidly diagnosing the case. 'By Jove, if he comes rotting about with me I'll kill him.' Having to do anything in a desperate hurry always made Charteris's temper slightly villainous. He turned the corner at a sharp trot, and came upon two youths who seemed to be engaged in the harmless occupation of trying to ride a bicycle. They were of the type which he held in especial aversion, the Rural Hooligan type, and one at least of the two had evidently been present at a recent circulation of the festive bowl. He was wheeling the bicycle about the road in an aimless manner, and looked as if he wondered what was the matter with it that it would not stay in the same place for two consecutive seconds. The other youth was apparently of the 'Charles-his-friend' variety, content to look on and applaud, and generally to play chorus to his companion's 'lead'. He was standing at the side of the road, smiling broadly in a way that argued feebleness of mind. Charteris was not quite sure which of the two types he loathed the more. He was inclined to call it a tie.

However, there seemed to be nothing particularly lawless in what they were doing now. If they were content to let him pass without hindrance, he, for his part, was content generously to overlook the insult they offered him in daring to exist, and to maintain a state of truce. But, as he drew nearer, he saw that there was more in this business than the casual spectator might at first have supposed. A second and keener inspection of the reptiles revealed fresh phenomena. In the first place, the bicycle which Hooligan number one was playing with was a lady's bicycle, and a small one at that. Now, up to the age of fourteen and the weight of ten stone, a beginner at cycling often finds it more convenient to learn to ride on a lady's machine than on a gentleman's. The former offers greater facilities for rapid dismounting, a quality not to be despised in the earlier stages of initiation. But, though this is undoubtedly the case, and though Charteris knew that it was so, yet he felt instinctively that there was something wrong here. Hooligans of twenty years and twelve stone do not learn to ride on small ladies' machines, or, if they do, it is probably without the permission of the small lady who owns the same. Valuable as his time was, Charteris felt that it behoved him to spend a thoughtful minute or so examining into this affair. He slowed down once again to a walk, and, as he did so, his eye fell upon the character in the drama whose absence had puzzled him, the owner of the bicycle. And from that moment he felt that life would be a hollow mockery if he failed to fall upon those revellers and slay them. She stood by the hedge on the right, a forlorn little figure in grey, and she gazed sadly and helplessly at the manoeuvres that were going on in the middle of the road. Her age Charteris put down at a venture at twelve—a correct guess. Her state of mind he also conjectured. She was letting 'I dare not' wait upon 'I would', like the late Macbeth, the cat i' the adage, and numerous other celebrities. She evidently had plenty of remarks to make on the subject in hand, but refrained from motives of prudence.

Charteris had no such scruples. The feeling of fatigue that had been upon him had vanished, and his temper, which had been growing steadily worse for some twenty minutes, now boiled over gleefully at the prospect of something solid to work itself off upon. Even without a cause Charteris detested the Rural Hooligan. Now that a real, copper-bottomed motive for this dislike had been supplied to him, he felt himself capable of dealing with a whole regiment of the breed. The criminal with the bicycle had just let it fall with a crash to the ground when Charteris went for him low, in the style which the Babe always insisted on seeing in members of the First Fifteen on the football field, and hove him without comment into a damp ditch. 'Charles his friend' uttered a shout of disapproval and rushed into the fray. Charteris gave him the straight left, of the type to which the great John Jackson is reported to have owed so much in the days of the old Prize Ring, and Charles, taking it between the eyes, stopped in a discouraged and discontented manner, and began to rub the place. Whereupon Charteris dashed in, and, to use an expression suitable to the deed, 'swung his right at the mark'. The 'mark', it may be explained for the benefit of the non-pugilistic, is that portion of the anatomy which lies hid behind the third button of the human waistcoat. It covers—in a most inadequate way—the wind, and even a gentle tap in the locality is apt to produce a fleeting sense of discomfort. A genuine flush hit on the spot, shrewdly administered by a muscular arm with the weight of the body behind it, causes the passive agent in the transaction to wish fervently, as far as he is at the moment physically capable of wishing anything, that he had never been born. 'Charles his friend' collapsed like an empty sack, and Charteris, getting a grip of the outlying portions of his costume, dragged him to the ditch and rolled him in on top of his friend, who had just recovered sufficiently to be thinking about getting out again. The pair of them lay there in a tangled heap. Charteris picked up the bicycle and gave it a cursory examination. The enamel was a good deal scratched, but no material damage had been done. He wheeled it across to its owner.

'It isn't much hurt,' he said, as they walked on slowly together. 'Bit scratched, that's all.'

'Thanks awfully,' said the small lady.

'Oh, not at all,' replied Charteris. 'I enjoyed it.' (He felt he had said the right thing there. Your real hero always 'enjoys it'.) 'I'm sorry those bargees frightened you.'

'They did rather. But'—she added triumphantly after a pause—'I didn't cry.'

'Rather not,' said Charteris. 'You were awfully plucky. I noticed. But hadn't you better ride on? Which way were you going?'

'I wanted to get to Stapleton.'

'Oh. That's simple enough. You've merely got to go straight on down this road, as straight as ever you can go. But, look here, you know, you shouldn't be out alone like this. It isn't safe. Why did they let you?'

The lady avoided his eye. She bent down and inspected the left pedal.

'They shouldn't have sent you out alone,' said Charteris, 'why did they?'

'They—they didn't. I came.'

There was a world of meaning in the phrase. Charteris felt that he was in the same case. They had not let him. He had come. Here was a kindred spirit, another revolutionary soul, scorning the fetters of convention and the so-called authority of self-constituted rules, aha! Bureaucrats!

'Shake hands,' he said, 'I'm in just the same way.'

They shook hands gravely.

'You know,' said the lady, 'I'm awfully sorry I did it now. It was very naughty.'

'I'm not sorry yet,' said Charteris, 'I'm rather glad than otherwise. But I expect I shall be sorry before long.'

'Will you be sent to bed?'

'I don't think so.'

'Will you have to learn beastly poetry?'

'Probably not.'

She looked at him curiously, as if to enquire, 'then if you won't have to learn poetry and you won't get sent to bed, what on earth is there for you to worry about?'

She would probably have gone on to investigate the problem further, but at that moment there came the sound of a whistle. Then another, closer this time. Then a faint rumbling, which increased in volume steadily. Charteris looked back. The railway line ran by the side of the road. He could see the smoke of a train through the trees. It was quite close now, and coming closer every minute, and he was still quite a hundred and fifty yards from the station gates.

'I say,' he cried. 'Great Scott, here comes my train. I must rush. Good-bye. You keep straight on.'

His legs had had time to grow stiff again. For the first few strides running was painful. But his joints soon adapted themselves to the strain, and in ten seconds he was sprinting as fast as he had ever sprinted off the running-track. When he had travelled a quarter of the distance the small cyclist overtook him.

'Be quick,' she said, 'it's just in sight.'

Charteris quickened his stride, and, paced by the bicycle, spun along in fine style. Forty yards from the station the train passed him. He saw it roll into the station. There were still twenty yards to go, exclusive of the station's steps, and he was already running as fast as it lay in him to run. Now there were only ten. Now five. And at last, with a hurried farewell to his companion, he bounded up the steps and on to the platform. At the end of the platform the line took a sharp curve to the left. Round that curve the tail end of the guard's van was just disappearing.

'Missed it, sir,' said the solitary porter, who managed things at Rutton, cheerfully. He spoke as if he was congratulating Charteris on having done something remarkably clever.

'When's the next?' panted Charteris.

'Eight-thirty,' was the porter's appalling reply.

For a moment Charteris felt quite ill. No train till eight-thirty! Then was he indeed lost. But it couldn't be true. There must be some sort of a train between now and then.

73

'Are you certain?' he said. 'Surely there's a train before that?'

'Why, yes, sir,' said the porter gleefully, 'but they be all exprusses. Eight-thirty be the only 'un what starps at Rootton.'

'Thanks,' said Charteris with marked gloom, 'I don't think that'll be much good to me. My aunt, what a hole I'm in.'

The porter made a sympathetic and interrogative noise at the back of his throat, as if inviting him to explain everything. But Charteris felt unequal to conversation. There are moments when one wants to be alone. He went down the steps again. When he got out into the road, his small cycling friend had vanished. Charteris was conscious of a feeling of envy towards her. She was doing the journey comfortably on a bicycle. He would have to walk it. Walk it! He didn't believe he could. The strangers' mile, followed by the Homeric combat with the two Hooligans and that ghastly sprint to wind up with, had left him decidedly unfit for further feats of pedestrianism. And it was eight miles to Stapleton, if it was a yard, and another mile from Stapleton to St Austin's. Charteris, having once more invoked the name of his aunt, pulled himself together with an effort, and limped gallantly on in the direction of Stapleton. But fate, so long hostile to him, at last relented. A rattle of wheels approached him from behind. A thrill of hope shot through him at the sound. There was the prospect of a lift. He stopped, and waited for the dog-cart—it sounded like a dog-cart—to arrive. Then he uttered a shout of rapture, and began to wave his arms like a semaphore. The man in the dog-cart was Dr Adamson.

'Hullo, Charteris,' said the Doctor, pulling up his horse, 'what are you doing here?'

'Give me a lift,' said Charteris, 'and I'll tell you. It's a long yarn. Can I get in?'

'Come along. Plenty of room.'

Charteris climbed up, and sank on to the cushioned seat with a sigh of pleasure. What glorious comfort. He had never enjoyed anything more in his life.

'I'm nearly dead,' he said, as the dog-cart went on again. 'This is how it all happened. You see, it was this way—'

And he embarked forthwith upon his narrative.

Chapter 6

By special request the Doctor dropped Charteris within a hundred yards of Merevale's door.

'Good-night,' he said. 'I don't suppose you will value my advice at all, but you may have it for what it is worth. I recommend you stop this sort of game. Next time something will happen.'

'By Jove, yes,' said Charteris, climbing painfully down from the dog-cart, 'I'll take that advice. I'm a reformed character from this day onwards. This sort of thing isn't good enough. Hullo, there's the bell for lock-up. Good-night, Doctor, and thanks most awfully for the lift. It was frightfully kind of you.'

'Don't mention it,' said Dr Adamson, 'it is always a privilege to be in your company. When are you coming to tea with me again?'

'Whenever you'll have me. I must get leave, though, this time.'

'Yes. By the way, how's Graham? It is Graham, isn't it? The fellow who broke his collar-bone?'

'Oh, he's getting on splendidly. Still in a sling, but it's almost well again now. But I must be off. Good-night.'

'Good-night. Come to tea next Monday.'

'Right,' said Charteris; 'thanks awfully.'

He hobbled in at Merevale's gate, and went up to his study. The Babe was in there talking to Welch.

'Hullo,' said the Babe, 'here's Charteris.'

'What's left of him,' said Charteris.

'How did it go off?'

'Don't, please.'

'Did you win?' asked Welch.

'No. Second. By a yard. Oh, Lord, I am dead.'

'Hot race?'

'Rather. It wasn't that, though. I had to sprint all the way to the station, and missed my train by ten seconds at the end of it all.'

'Then how did you get here?'

'That was the one stroke of luck I've had this afternoon. I started to walk back, and after I'd gone about a quarter of a mile, Adamson caught me up in his dog-cart. I suggested that it would be a Christian act on his part to give me a lift, and he did. I shall remember Adamson in my will.'

'Tell us what happened.'

'I'll tell thee everything I can,' said Charteris. 'There's little to relate. I saw an aged, aged man a-sitting on a gate. Where do you want me to begin?'

'At the beginning. Don't rot.'

'I was born,' began Charteris, 'of poor but honest parents, who sent me to school at an early age in order that I might acquire a grasp of the Greek and Latin languages, now obsolete. I—'

'How did you lose?' enquired the Babe.

'The other man beat me. If he hadn't, I should have won hands down. Oh, I say, guess who I met at Rutton.'

'Not a beak?'

'No. Almost as bad, though. The Bargee man who paced me from Stapleton. Man who crocked Tony.'

75

'Great Scott!' cried the Babe. 'Did he recognize you?'

'Rather. We had a very pleasant conversation.'

'If he reports you,' began the Babe.

'Who's that?'

Charteris looked up. Tony Graham had entered the study.

'Hullo, Tony! Adamson told me to remember him to you.'

'So you've got back?'

Charteris confirmed the hasty guess.

'But what are you talking about, Babe?' said Tony. 'Who's going to be reported, and who's going to report?'

The Babe briefly explained the situation.

'If the man,' he said, 'reports Charteris, he may get run in tomorrow, and then we shall have both our halves away against Dacre's. Charteris, you are a fool to go rotting about out of bounds like this.'

'Nay, dry the starting tear,' said Charteris cheerfully. 'In the first place, I shouldn't get kept in on a Thursday anyhow. I should be shoved into extra on Saturday. Also, I shrewdly conveyed to the Bargee the impression that I was at Rutton by special permission.'

'He's bound to know that that can't be true,' said Tony.

'Well, I told him to think it over. You see, he got so badly left last time he tried to compass my downfall, that I shouldn't be a bit surprised if he let the job alone this journey.'

'Let's hope so,' said the Babe gloomily.

'That's right, Babby,' remarked Charteris encouragingly, nodding at the pessimist.

'You buck up and keep looking on the bright side. It'll be all right. You see if it won't. If there's any running in to be done, I shall do it. I shall be frightfully fit tomorrow after all this dashing about today. I haven't an ounce of superfluous flesh on me. I'm a fine, strapping specimen of sturdy young English manhood. And I'm going to play a very selfish game tomorrow, Babe.'

'Oh, my dear chap, you mustn't.' The Babe's face wore an expression of horror. The success of the House-team in the final was very near to his heart. He could not understand anyone jesting on the subject. Charteris respected his anguish, and relieved it speedily.

'I was only ragging,' he said. 'Considering that our three-quarter line is our one strong point, I'm not likely to keep the ball from it, if I get a chance of getting it out. Make your mind easy, Babe.'

The final House-match was always a warmish game. The rivalry between the various Houses was great, and the football cup especially was fought for with immense keenness. Also, the match

76

was the last fixture of the season, and there was a certain feeling in the teams that if they did happen to disable a man or two, it would not matter much. The injured sportsman would not be needed for School-match purposes for another six months. As a result of which philosophical reflection, the tackling was ruled slightly energetic, and the handing-off was done with vigour.

This year, to add a sort of finishing touch, there was just a little ill-feeling between Dacre's and Merevale's. The cause of it was the Babe. Until the beginning of the term he had been a day boy. Then the news began to circulate that he was going to become a boarder, either at Dacre's or at Merevale's. He chose the latter, and Dacre's felt slightly aggrieved. Some of the less sportsmanlike members of the House had proposed that a protest should be made against his being allowed to play, but, fortunately for the credit of Dacre's, Prescott, the captain of the House Fifteen, had put his foot down with an emphatic bang at the suggestion. As he sagely pointed out, there were some things which were bad form, and this was one of them. If the team wanted to express their disapproval, said he, let them do it on the field by tackling their very hardest. He personally was going to do his best, and he advised them to do the same.

The rumour of this bad blood had got about the School in some mysterious manner, and when Swift, Merevale's only First Fifteen forward, kicked off up the hill, a large crowd was lining the ropes. It was evident from the outset that it would be a good game.

Dacre's were the better side—as a team. They had no really weak spot. But Merevale's extraordinarily strong three-quarter line somewhat made up for an inferior scrum. And the fact that the Babe was in the centre was worth much.

At first Dacre's pressed. Their pack was unusually heavy for a House-team, and they made full use of it. They took the ball down the field in short rushes till they were in Merevale's twenty-five. Then they began to heel, and, if things had been more or less exciting for the Merevalians before, they became doubly so now. The ground was dry, and so was the ball, and the game consequently waxed fast. Time after time the ball went along Dacre's three-quarter line, only to end by finding itself hurled, with the wing who was carrying it, into touch. Occasionally the centres, instead of feeding their wings, would try to dodge through themselves. And that was where the Babe came in. He was admittedly the best tackler in the School, but on this occasion he excelled himself. His man never had a chance of getting past. At last a lofty kick into touch over the heads of the spectators gave the players a few seconds' rest.

The Babe went up to Charteris.

'Look here,' he said, 'it's risky, but I think we'll try having the ball out a bit.'

'In our own twenty-five?' said Charteris.

'Wherever we are. I believe it will come off all right. Anyway, we'll try it. Tell the forwards.'

For forwards playing against a pack much heavier than themselves, it is easier to talk about letting the ball out than to do it. The first half dozen times that Merevale's scrum tried to heel they were shoved off their feet, and it was on the enemy's side that the ball went out. But the seventh attempt succeeded. Out it came, cleanly and speedily. Daintree, who was playing instead of Tony, switched it across to Charteris. Charteris dodged the half who was marking him, and ran. Heeling and passing in one's own twenty-five is like smoking—an excellent practice if indulged in in moderation. On this occasion it answered perfectly. Charteris ran to the half-way line, and handed the ball on to the Babe. The Babe was tackled from behind, and passed to Thomson. Thomson dodged his man, and passed to Welch on the wing. Welch was the fastest sprinter in the School. It was a pleasure—if you did not happen to be one of the opposing side—to see him race down the touch-line. He was off like an arrow. Dacre's back made a futile attempt to get at him. Welch could have given the back fifteen yards in a hundred. He ran round him, and, amidst terrific applause from the Merevale's-supporting section of the audience, scored between the posts. The Babe took the kick and converted without difficulty. Five minutes afterwards the whistle blew for half-time.

The remainder of the game does not call for detailed description. Dacre's pressed nearly the whole of the last half hour, but twice more the ball came out and went down Merevale's three-quarter line. Once it was the Babe who scored with a run from his own goal-line, and once Charteris, who got in from half-way, dodging through the whole team. The last ten minutes of the game was marked by a slight excess of energy on both sides. Dacre's forwards were in a decidedly bad temper, and fought like tigers to break through, and Merevale's played up to them with spirit. The Babe seemed continually to be precipitating himself at the feet of rushing forwards, and Charteris felt as if at least a dozen bones were broken in various portions of his anatomy. The game ended on Merevale's line, but they had won the match and the cup by two goals and a try to nothing.

Charteris limped off the field, cheerful but damaged. He ached all over, and there was a large bruise on his left cheek-bone. He and

Babe were going to the House, when they were aware that the Headmaster was beckoning to them.

'Well, MacArthur, and what was the result of the match?'

'We won, sir,' boomed the Babe. 'Two goals and a try to nil.'

'You have hurt your cheek, Charteris?'

'Yes, sir.'

'How did you do that?'

'I got a kick, sir, in one of the rushes.'

'Ah. I should bathe it, Charteris. Bathe it well. I hope it will not be very painful. Bathe it well in warm water.'

He walked on.

'You know,' said Charteris to the Babe, as they went into the House, 'the Old Man isn't such a bad sort after all. He has his points, don't you think?'

The Babe said that he did.

'I'm going to reform, you know,' continued Charteris confidentially.

'It's about time,' said the Babe. 'You can have the bath first if you like. Only buck up.'

Charteris boiled himself for ten minutes, and then dragged his weary limbs to his study. It was while he was sitting in a deck-chair eating mixed biscuits, and wondering if he would ever be able to summon up sufficient energy to put on garments of civilization, that somebody knocked at the door.

'Yes,' shouted Charteris. 'What is it? Don't come in. I'm changing.'

The melodious treble of Master Crowinshaw, his fag, made itself heard through the keyhole.

'The Head told me to tell you that he wanted to see you at the School House as soon as you can go.'

'All right,' shouted Charteris. 'Thanks.'

'Now what,' he continued to himself, 'does the Old Man want to see me for? Perhaps he wants to make certain that I've bathed my cheek in warm water. Anyhow, I suppose I must go.'

A quarter of an hour later he presented himself at the Headmagisterial door. The sedate Parker, the Head's butler, who always filled Charteris with a desire to dig him hard in the ribs just to see what would happen, ushered him into the study.

The Headmaster was reading by the light of a lamp when Charteris came in. He laid down his book, and motioned him to a seat; after which there was an awkward pause.

'I have just received,' began the Head at last, 'a most unpleasant communication. Most unpleasant. From whom it comes

I do not know. It is, in fact—er—anonymous. I am sorry that I ever read it.'

He stopped. Charteris made no comment. He guessed what was coming. He, too, was sorry that the Head had ever read the letter.

'The writer says that he saw you, that he actually spoke to you, at the athletic sports at Rutton yesterday. I have called you in to tell me if that is true.' The Head fastened an accusing eye on his companion.

'It is quite true, sir,' said Charteris steadily.

'What!' said the Head sharply. 'You were at Rutton?'

'Yes, sir.'

'You were perfectly aware, I suppose, that you were breaking the School rules by going there, Charteris?' enquired the Head in a cold voice.

'Yes, sir.' There was another pause.

'This is very serious,' began the Head. 'I cannot overlook this. I—'

There was a slight scuffle of feet in the passage outside. The door flew open vigorously, and a young lady entered. It was, as Charteris recognized in a minute, his acquaintance of the afternoon, the young lady of the bicycle.

'Uncle,' she said, 'have you seen my book anywhere?'

'Hullo!' she broke off as her eye fell on Charteris.

'Hullo!' said Charteris, affably, not to be outdone in the courtesies.

'Did you catch your train?'

'No. Missed it.'

'Hullo! what's the matter with your cheek?'

'I got a kick on it.'

'Oh, does it hurt?'

'Not much, thanks.'

Here the Head, feeling perhaps a little out of it, put in his oar.

'Dorothy, you must not come here now. I am busy. And how, may I ask, do you and Charteris come to be acquainted?'

'Why, he's him,' said Dorothy lucidly.

The Head looked puzzled.

'Him. The chap, you know.'

It is greatly to the Head's credit that he grasped the meaning of these words. Long study of the classics had quickened his faculty for seeing sense in passages where there was none. The situation dawned upon him.

'Do you mean to tell me, Dorothy, that it was Charteris who came to your assistance yesterday?'

Dorothy nodded energetically.

'He gave the men beans,' she said. 'He did, really,' she went on, regardless of the Head's look of horror. 'He used right and left with considerable effect.'

Dorothy's brother, a keen follower of the Ring, had been good enough some days before to read her out an extract from an account in The Sportsman of a match at the National Sporting Club, and the account had been much to her liking. She regarded it as a masterpiece of English composition.

'Dorothy,' said the Headmaster, 'run away to bed.' A suggestion which she treated with scorn, it wanting a clear two hours to her legal bedtime. 'I must speak to your mother about your deplorable habit of using slang. Dear me, I must certainly speak to her.'

And, shamefully unabashed, Dorothy retired.

The Head was silent for a few minutes after she had gone; then he turned to Charteris again.

'In consideration of this, Charteris, I shall—er—mitigate slightly the punishment I had intended to give you.'

Charteris murmured his gratification.

'But,' continued the Head sternly, 'I cannot overlook the offence. I have my duty to consider. You will therefore write me—er—ten lines of Virgil by tomorrow evening, Charteris.'

'Yes, sir.'

'Latin and English,' said the relentless pedagogue.

'Yes, sir.'

'And, Charteris—I am speaking now—er—unofficially, not as a headmaster, you understand—if in future you would cease to break School rules simply as a matter of principle, for that, I fancy, is what it amounts to, I—er—well, I think we should get on better together. And that is, on my part at least, a consummation—er—devoutly to be wished. Good-night, Charteris.'

'Good-night, sir.'

The Head extended a large hand. Charteris took it, and his departure.

The Headmaster opened his book again, and turned over a new leaf. Charteris at the same moment, walking slowly in the direction of Merevale's, was resolving for the future to do the very same thing. And he did.

81

9

HOW PAYNE BUCKED UP

I

It was Walkinshaw's affair from the first. Grey, the captain of the St Austin's Fifteen, was in the infirmary nursing a bad knee. To him came Charles Augustus Walkinshaw with a scheme. Walkinshaw was football secretary, and in Grey's absence acted as captain. Besides these two there were only a couple of last year's team left—Reade and Barrett, both of Philpott's House.

'Hullo, Grey, how's the knee?' said Walkinshaw.

'How's the team getting on?' he said.

'Well, as far as I can see,' said Walkinshaw, 'we ought to have a rather good season, if you'd only hurry up and come back. We beat a jolly hot lot of All Comers yesterday. Smith was playing for them. The Blue, you know. And lots of others. We got a goal and a try to nil.'

'Good,' said Grey. 'Who did anything for us? Who scored?'

'I got in once. Payne got the other.'

'By Jove, did he? What sort of a game is he playing this year?'

The moment had come for Walkinshaw to unburden himself to his scheme. He proceeded to do so.

'Not up to much,' he said. 'Look here, Grey, I've got rather an idea. It's my opinion Payne's not bucking up nearly as much as he might. Do you mind if I leave him out of the next game?'

Grey stared. The idea was revolutionary.

'What! Leave him out? My good man, he'll be the next chap to get his colours. He's a cert. for his cap.'

'That's just it. He knows he's a cert., and he's slacking on the strength of it. Now, my idea is that if you slung him out for a match or two, he'd buck up extra hard when he came into the team again. Can't I have a shot at it?'

Grey weighed the matter. Walkinshaw pressed home his arguments.

'You see, it isn't like cricket. At cricket, of course, it might put a chap off awfully to be left out, but I don't see how it can hurt a man's play at footer. Besides, he's beginning to stick on side already.'

'Is he, by Jove?' said Grey. This was the unpardonable sin.

82

'Well, I'll tell you what you can do if you like. Get up a scratch game, First Fifteen v. Second, and make him captain of the Second.'

'Right,' said Walkinshaw, and retired beaming.

Walkinshaw, it may be remarked at once, to prevent mistakes, was a well-meaning idiot. There was no doubt about his being well-meaning. Also, there was no doubt about his being an idiot. He was continually getting insane ideas into his head, and being unable to get them out again. This matter of Payne was a good example of his customary methods. He had put his hand on the one really first-class forward St Austin's possessed, and proposed to remove him from the team. And yet through it all he was perfectly well-meaning. The fact that personally he rather disliked Payne had, to do him justice, no weight at all with him. He would have done the same by his bosom friend under like circumstances. This is the only excuse that can be offered for him. It was true that Payne regarded himself as a certainty for his colours, as far as anything can be considered certain in this vale of sorrow. But to accuse him of trading on this, and, to use the vernacular, of putting on side, was unjust to a degree.

On the afternoon following this conversation Payne, who was a member of Dacre's House, came into his study and banged his books down on the table with much emphasis. This was a sign that he was feeling dissatisfied with the way in which affairs were conducted in the world. Bowden, who was asleep in an armchair— he had been staying in with a cold—woke with a start. Bowden shared Payne's study. He played centre three-quarter for the Second Fifteen.

'Hullo!' he said.

Payne grunted. Bowden realized that matters had not been going well with him. He attempted to soothe him with conversation, choosing what he thought would be a congenial topic.

'What's on on Saturday?' he asked.

'Scratch game. First v. Second.'

Bowden groaned.

'I know those First v. Second games,' he said. 'They turn the Second out to get butchered for thirty-five minutes each way, to improve the First's combination. It may be fun for the First, but it's not nearly so rollicking for us. Look here, Payne, if you find me with the pill at any time, you can let me down easy, you know. You needn't go bringing off any of your beastly gallery tackles.'

'I won't,' said Payne. 'To start with, it would be against rules. We happen to be on the same side.'

'Rot, man; I'm not playing for the First.' This was the only explanation that occurred to him.

'I'm playing for the Second.'

'What! Are you certain?'

'I've seen the list. They're playing Babington instead of me.'

'But why? Babington's no good.'

'I think they have a sort of idea I'm slacking or something. At any rate, Walkinshaw told me that if I bucked up I might get tried again.'

'Silly goat,' said Bowden. 'What are you going to do?'

'I'm going to take his advice, and buck up.'

II

He did. At the beginning of the game the ropes were lined by some thirty spectators, who had come to derive a languid enjoyment from seeing the First pile up a record score. By half-time their numbers had risen to an excited mob of something over three hundred, and the second half of the game was fought out to the accompaniment of a storm of yells and counter yells such as usually only belonged to school-matches. The Second Fifteen, after a poor start, suddenly awoke to the fact that this was not going to be the conventional massacre by any means. The First had scored an unconverted try five minutes after the kick-off, and it was after this that the Second began to get together. The school back bungled the drop out badly, and had to find touch in his own twenty-five, and after that it was anyone's game. The scrums were a treat to behold. Payne was a monument of strength. Time after time the Second had the ball out to their three-quarters, and just after half-time Bowden slipped through in the corner. The kick failed, and the two teams, with their scores equal now, settled down grimly to fight the thing out to a finish. But though they remained on their opponents' line for most of the rest of the game, the Second did not add to their score, and the match ended in a draw of three points all.

The first intimation Grey received of this came to him late in the evening. He had been reading a novel which, whatever its other merits may have been, was not interesting, and it had sent him to sleep. He awoke to hear a well-known voice observe with some unction: 'Ah! M'yes. Leeches and hot fomentations.' This effectually banished sleep. If there were two things in the world that he loathed, they were leeches and hot fomentations, and the School doctor apparently regarded them as a panacea for every kind of bodily ailment, from a fractured skull to a cold in the head. It was this gentleman who had just spoken, but Grey's alarm vanished as he perceived that the words had no personal application to himself. The object of the remark was a fellow-sufferer in the next bed but one. Now Grey was certain that when he had fallen asleep there had been nobody in that bed. When, therefore, the medical expert had departed on his fell errand, the quest of leeches and hot fomentations, he sat up and gave tongue.

'Who's that in that bed?' he asked.

'Hullo, Grey,' replied a voice. 'Didn't know you were awake. I've come to keep you company.'

'That you, Barrett? What's up with you?'

'Collar-bone. Dislocated it or something. Reade's over in that corner. He has bust his ankle. Oh, yes, we've been having a nice, cheery afternoon,' concluded Barrett bitterly.

'Great Scott! How did it happen?'

'Payne.'

'Where? In your collar-bone?'

'Yes. That wasn't what I meant, though. What I was explaining was that Payne got hold of me in the middle of the field, and threw me into touch. After which he fell on me. That was enough for my simple needs. I'm not grasping.'

'How about Reade?'

'The entire Second scrum collapsed on top of Reade. When we dug him out his ankle was crocked. Mainspring gone, probably. Then they gathered up the pieces and took them gently away. I don't know how it all ended.'

Just then Walkinshaw burst into the room. He had a large bruise over one eye, his arm was in a sling, and he limped. But he was in excellent spirits.

'I knew I was right, by Jove,' he observed to Grey. 'I knew he could buck up if he liked.'

'I know it now,' said Barrett.

'Who's this you're talking about?' said Grey.

'Payne. I've never seen anything like the game he played today. He was everywhere. And, by Jove, his tackling!'

'Don't,' said Barrett, wearily.

'It's the best match I ever played in,' said Walkinshaw, bubbling over with enthusiasm. 'Do you know, the Second had all the best of the game.'

'What was the score?'

'Draw. One try all.'

'And now I suppose you're satisfied?' enquired Barrett. The

great scheme for the regeneration of Payne had been confided to him by its proud patentee.

'Almost,' said Walkinshaw. 'We'll continue the treatment for one more game, and then we'll have him simply fizzing for the Windybury match. That's next Saturday. By the way, I'm afraid you'll hardly be fit again in time for that, Barrett, will you?'

'I may possibly,' said Barrett, coldly, 'be getting about again in time for the Windybury match of the year after next. This year I'm afraid I shall not have the pleasure. And I should strongly advise you, if you don't want to have to put a team of cripples into the field, to discontinue the treatment, as you call it.'

'Oh, I don't know,' said Walkinshaw.

On the following Wednesday evening, at five o'clock, something was carried in on a stretcher, and deposited in the bed which lay between Grey and Barrett. Close scrutiny revealed the fact that it was what had once been Charles Augustus Walkinshaw. He was slightly broken up.

'Payne?' enquired Grey in chilly tones.

Walkinshaw admitted the impeachment.

Grey took a pencil and a piece of paper from the table at his side. 'If you want to know what I'm doing,' he said, 'I'm writing out the team for the Windybury match, and I'm going to make Payne captain, as the senior Second Fifteen man. And if we win I'm jolly well going to give him his cap after the match. If we don't win, it'll be the fault of a raving lunatic of the name of Walkinshaw, with his beastly Colney Hatch schemes for reforming slack forwards. You utter rotter!'

Fortunately for the future peace of mind of C. A. Walkinshaw, the latter contingency did not occur. The School, in spite of its absentees, contrived to pull the match off by a try to nil. Payne, as was only right and proper, scored the try, making his way through the ranks of the visiting team with the quiet persistence of a steam-roller. After the game he came to tea, by request, at the infirmary, and was straightaway invested by Grey with his First Fifteen colours. On his arrival he surveyed the invalids with interest.

'Rough game, footer,' he observed at length.

'Don't mention it,' said Barrett politely. 'Leeches,' he added dreamily. 'Leeches and hot fomentations. Boiling fomentations. Will somebody kindly murder Walkinshaw!'

'Why?' asked Payne, innocently.

10

AUTHOR!

J. S. M. Babington, of Dacre's House, was on the horns of a dilemma. Circumstances over which he had had no control had brought him, like another Hercules, to the cross-roads, and had put before him the choice between pleasure and duty, or, rather, between pleasure and what those in authority called duty. Being human, he would have had little difficulty in making his decision, had not the path of pleasure been so hedged about by danger as to make him doubt whether after all the thing could be carried through.

The facts in the case were these. It was the custom of the mathematical set to which J. S. M. Babington belonged, 4B to wit, to relieve the tedium of the daily lesson with a species of round game which was played as follows. As soon as the master had taken his seat, one of the players would execute a manoeuvre calculated to draw attention on himself, such as dropping a book or upsetting the blackboard. Called up to the desk to give explanation, he would embark on an eloquent speech for the defence. This was the cue for the next player to begin. His part consisted in making his way to the desk and testifying to the moral excellence of his companion, and giving in full the reasons why he should be discharged without a stain upon his character. As soon as he had warmed to his work he would be followed by a third player, and so on until the standing room around the desk was completely filled with a great cloud of witnesses. The duration of the game varied, of course, considerably. On some occasions it could be played through with such success, that the master would enter into the spirit of the thing, and do his best to book the names of all offenders at one and the same time, a feat of no inconsiderable difficulty. At other times matters would come to a head more rapidly. In any case, much innocent fun was to be derived from it, and its popularity was great. On the day, however, on which this story opens, a new master had been temporarily loosed into the room in place of the Rev. Septimus Brown, who had been there as long as the oldest inhabitant could remember. The Rev. Septimus was a wrangler, but knew nothing of the ways of the human boy. His successor, Mr. Reginald Seymour, was a poor mathematician, but a good master. He had been, moreover, a Cambridge Rugger Blue. This fact alone should have ensured him against the customary pleasantries, for a Blue is a man to be respected. It was not only injudicious, therefore, but positively wrong of Babington to plunge against the blackboard on his way to his place. If he had been a student of Tennyson, he might have remembered that the old order is in the habit of changing and yielding place to the new.

Mr. Seymour looked thoughtfully for a moment at the blackboard.

'That was rather a crude effort,' he said pleasantly to Babington, 'you lack finesse. Pick it up again, please.'

Babington picked it up without protest. Under the rule of the Rev. Septimus this would have been the signal for the rest of the class to leave their places and assist him, but now they seemed to realize that there was a time for everything, and that this was decidedly no time for indoor games.

'Thank you,' said Mr. Seymour, when the board was in its place again. 'What is your name? Eh, what? I didn't quite hear.'

'Babington, sir.'

'Ah. You had better come in tomorrow at two and work out examples three hundred to three-twenty in "Hall and Knight". There is really plenty of room to walk in between that desk and the blackboard. It only wants practice.'

What was left of Babington then went to his seat. He felt that his reputation as an artistic player of the game had received a shattering blow. Then there was the imposition. This in itself would have troubled him little. To be kept in on a half-holiday is annoying, but it is one of those ills which the flesh is heir to, and your true philosopher can always take his gruel like a man.

But it so happened that by the evening post he had received a letter from a cousin of his, who was a student at Guy's, and from all accounts was building up a great reputation in the medical world. From this letter it appeared that by a complicated process of knowing people who knew other people who had influence with the management, he had contrived to obtain two tickets for a morning performance of the new piece that had just been produced at one of the theatres. And if Mr. J. S. M. Babington wished to avail himself of the opportunity, would he write by return, and be at Charing Cross Underground bookstall at twenty past two.

Now Babington, though he objected strongly to the drama of ancient Greece, was very fond of that of the present day, and he registered a vow that if the matter could possibly be carried through, it should be. His choice was obvious. He could cut his engagement with Mr. Seymour, or he could keep it. The difficulty lay rather in deciding upon one or other of the alternatives. The whole thing turned upon the extent of the penalty in the event of detection.

That was his dilemma. He sought advice.

'I should risk it,' said his bosom friend Peterson.

'I shouldn't advise you to,' remarked Jenkins.

Jenkins was equally a bosom friend, and in the matter of wisdom in no way inferior to Peterson.

'What would happen, do you think?' asked Babington.

'Sack,' said one authority.

'Jaw, and double impot,' said another.

'The Daily Telegraph,' muttered the tempter in a stage aside, 'calls it the best comedy since Sheridan.'

'So it does,' thought Babington. 'I'll risk it.'

'You'll be a fool if you do,' croaked the gloomy Jenkins. 'You're bound to be caught.' But the Ayes had it. Babington wrote off that night accepting the invitation.

It was with feelings of distinct relief that he heard Mr. Seymour express to another master his intention of catching the twelve-fifteen train up to town. It meant that he would not be on the scene to see him start on the 'Hall and Knight'. Unless luck were very much against him, Babington might reasonably hope that he would accept the imposition without any questions. He had taken the precaution to get the examples finished overnight, with the help of Peterson and Jenkins, aided by a weird being who actually appeared to like algebra, and turned out ten of the twenty problems in an incredibly short time in exchange for a couple of works of fiction (down) and a tea (at a date). He himself meant to catch the one-thirty, which would bring him to town in good time. Peterson had promised to answer his name at roll-call, a delicate operation, in which long practice had made him, like many others of the junior members of the House, no mean proficient.

It would be pleasant for a conscientious historian to be able to say that the one-thirty broke down just outside Victoria, and that Babington arrived at the theatre at the precise moment when the curtain fell and the gratified audience began to stream out. But truth, though it crush me. The one-thirty was so punctual that one might have thought that it belonged to a line other than the line to which it did belong. From Victoria to Charing Cross is a journey that occupies no considerable time, and Babington found himself at his destination with five minutes to wait. At twenty past his cousin arrived, and they made their way to the theatre. A brief skirmish with a liveried menial in the lobby, and they were in their seats.

Some philosopher, of extraordinary powers of intuition, once informed the world that the best of things come at last to an end. The statement was tested, and is now universally accepted as correct. To apply the general to the particular, the play came to an end amidst uproarious applause, to which Babington contributed an unstinted quotum, about three hours after it had begun.

'What do you say to going and grubbing somewhere?' asked Babington's cousin, as they made their way out.

'Hullo, there's that man Richards,' he continued, before Babington could reply that of all possible actions he considered that of going and grubbing somewhere the most desirable. 'Fellow I know at Guy's, you know,' he added, in explanation. 'I'll get him to join us. You'll like him, I expect.'

Richards professed himself delighted, and shook hands with Babington with a fervour which seemed to imply that until he had met him life had been a dreary blank, but that now he could begin to enjoy himself again. 'I should like to join you, if you don't mind including a friend of mine in the party,' said Richards. 'He was to meet me here. By the way, he's the author of that new piece—The Way of the World.'

'Why, we've just been there.'

'Oh, then you will probably like to meet him. Here he is.'

As he spoke a man came towards them, and, with a shock that sent all the blood in his body to the very summit of his head, and then to the very extremities of his boots, Babington recognized Mr. Seymour. The assurance of the programme that the play was by Walter Walsh was a fraud. Nay worse, a downright and culpable lie. He started with the vague idea of making a rush for safety, but before his paralysed limbs could be induced to work, Mr. Seymour had arrived, and he was being introduced (oh, the tragic irony of it) to the man for whose benefit he was at that very moment supposed to be working out examples three hundred to three-twenty in 'Hall and Knight'.

Mr. Seymour shook hands, without appearing to recognize him. Babington's blood began to resume its normal position again, though he felt that this seeming ignorance of his identity might be a mere veneer, a wile of guile, as the bard puts it. He remembered, with a pang, a story in some magazine where a prisoner was subjected to what the light-hearted inquisitors called the torture of hope. He was allowed to escape from prison, and pass guards and sentries apparently without their noticing him. Then, just as he stepped into the open air, the chief inquisitor tapped him gently on the shoulder, and, more in sorrow than in anger, reminded him that it was customary for condemned men to remain inside their cells. Surely this was a similar case. But then the thought came to him that Mr. Seymour had only seen him once, and so might possibly have failed to remember him, for there was nothing special about Babington's features that arrested the eye, and stamped them on the brain for all time. He was rather ordinary than otherwise to look at. At tea, as bad luck would have it, the two sat opposite one another, and Babington trembled. Then the worst happened. Mr. Seymour, who had been looking attentively at him for some time, leaned forward and said in a tone evidently devoid of suspicion: 'Haven't we met before somewhere? I seem to remember your face.'

'Er—no, no,' replied Babington. 'That is, I think not. We may have.'

'I feel sure we have. What school are you at?'

Babington's soul began to writhe convulsively.

'What, what school? Oh, what school? Why, er—I'm at—er—Uppingham.'

Mr. Seymour's face assumed a pleased expression.

'Uppingham? Really. Why, I know several Uppingham fellows. Do you know Mr. Morton? He's a master at Uppingham, and a great friend of mine.'

The room began to dance briskly before Babington's eyes, but he clutched at a straw, or what he thought was a straw.

'Uppingham? Did I say Uppingham? Of course, I mean Rugby, you know, Rugby. One's always mixing the two up, you know. Isn't one?'

Mr. Seymour looked at him in amazement. Then he looked at the others as if to ask which of the two was going mad, he or the youth opposite him. Babington's cousin listened to the wild fictions which issued from his lips in equal amazement. He thought he must be ill. Even Richards had a fleeting impression that it was a little odd that a fellow should forget what school he was at, and mistake the name Rugby for that of Uppingham, or vice versa. Babington became an object of interest.

'I say, Jack,' said the cousin, 'you're feeling all right, aren't you? I mean, you don't seem to know what you're talking about. If you're going to be ill, say so, and I'll prescribe for you.'

'Is he at Rugby?' asked Mr. Seymour.

'No, of course he's not. How could he have got from Rugby to London in time for a morning performance? Why, he's at St Austin's.'

Mr. Seymour sat for a moment in silence, taking this in. Then he chuckled. 'It's all right,' he said, 'he's not ill. We have met before, but under such painful circumstances that Master Babington very thoughtfully dissembled, in order not to remind me of them.'

He gave a brief synopsis of what had occurred. The audience, exclusive of Babington, roared with laughter.

'I suppose,' said the cousin, 'you won't prosecute, will you? It's really such shocking luck, you know, that you ought to forget you're a master.'

Mr. Seymour stirred his tea and added another lump of sugar very carefully before replying. Babington watched him in silence, and wished that he would settle the matter quickly, one way or the other.

'Fortunately for Babington,' said Mr. Seymour, 'and unfortunately for the cause of morality, I am not a master. I was only a stop-gap, and my term of office ceased today at one o'clock. Thus the prisoner at the bar gets off on a technical point of law, and I trust it will be a lesson to him. I suppose you had the sense to do the imposition?'

'Yes, sir, I sat up last night.'

'Good. Now, if you'll take my advice, you'll reform, or another day you'll come to a bad end. By the way, how did you manage about roll-call today?'

'I thought that was an awfully good part just at the end of the first act,' said Babington.

Mr. Seymour smiled. Possibly from gratification.

'Well, how did it go off?' asked Peterson that night.

'Don't, old chap,' said Babington, faintly.

'I told you so,' said Jenkins at a venture.

But when he had heard the whole story he withdrew the remark, and commented on the wholly undeserved good luck some people seemed to enjoy.

11

'THE TABBY TERROR'

The struggle between Prater's cat and Prater's cat's conscience was short, and ended in the hollowest of victories for the former. The conscience really had no sort of chance from the beginning. It was weak by nature and flabby from long want of exercise, while the cat was in excellent training, and was, moreover, backed up by a strong temptation. It pocketed the stakes, which consisted of most of the contents of a tin of sardines, and left unostentatiously by the window. When Smith came in after football, and found the remains, he was surprised, and even pained. When Montgomery entered soon afterwards, he questioned him on the subject.

'I say, have you been having a sort of preliminary canter with the banquet?'

'No,' said Montgomery. 'Why?'

'Somebody has,' said Smith, exhibiting the empty tin. 'Doesn't seem to have had such a bad appetite, either.'

'This reminds me of the story of the great bear, the medium bear, and the little ditto,' observed Montgomery, who was apt at an analogy. 'You may remember that when the great bear found his porridge tampered with, he—'

At this point Shawyer entered. He had been bidden to the feast, and was feeling ready for it.

'Hullo, tea ready?' he asked.

Smith displayed the sardine tin in much the same manner as the conjurer shows a pack of cards when he entreats you to choose one, and remember the number.

'You haven't finished already, surely? Why, it's only just five.'

'We haven't even begun,' said Smith. 'That's just the difficulty. The question is, who has been on the raid in here?'

'No human being has done this horrid thing,' said Montgomery. He always liked to introduce a Holmes-Watsonian touch into the conversation. 'In the first place, the door was locked, wasn't it, Smith?'

'By Jove, so it was. Then how on earth—?'

'Through the window, of course. The cat, equally of course. I should like a private word with that cat.'

'I suppose it must have been.'

'Of course it was. Apart from the merely circumstantial evidence, which is strong enough to hang it off its own bat, we have absolute proof of its guilt. Just cast your eye over that butter. You follow me, Watson?'

The butter was submitted to inspection. In the very centre of it there was a footprint.

'I traced his little footprints in the butter,' said Montgomery. 'Now, is that the mark of a human foot?'

The jury brought in a unanimous verdict of guilty against the missing animal, and over a sorrowful cup of tea, eked out with bread and jam—butter appeared to be unpopular—discussed the matter in all its bearings. The cat had not been an inmate of Prater's House for a very long time, and up till now what depredation it had committed had been confined to the official larder. Now, however, it had evidently got its hand in, and was about to commence operations upon a more extensive scale. The Tabby Terror had begun. Where would it end? The general opinion was that something would have to be done about it. No one seemed to know exactly what to do. Montgomery spoke darkly of bricks, bits of string, and horse-ponds. Smith rolled the word 'rat-poison' luxuriously round his tongue. Shawyer, who was something of an expert on the range, babbled of air-guns.

At tea on the following evening the first really serious engagement of the campaign took place. The cat strolled into the tea-room in the patronizing way characteristic of his kind, but was heavily shelled with lump-sugar, and beat a rapid retreat. That was the signal for the outbreak of serious hostilities. From that moment its paw was against every man, and the tale of the things it stole is too terrible to relate in detail. It scored all along the line. Like Death in the poem, it knocked at the doors of the highest and the lowest alike. Or rather, it did not exactly knock. It came in without knocking. The palace of the prefect and the hovel of the fag suffered equally. Trentham, the head of the House, lost sausages to an incredible amount one evening, and the next day Ripton, of the Lower Third, was robbed of his one ewe lamb in the shape of half a tin of anchovy paste. Panic reigned.

It was after this matter of the sausages that a luminous idea occurred to Trentham. He had been laid up with a slight football accident, and his family, reading between the lines of his written statement that he 'had got crocked at footer, nothing much, only (rather a nuisance) might do him out of the House-matches', a notification of mortal injuries, and seeming to hear a death-rattle through the words 'felt rather chippy yesterday', had come down en masse to investigate. En masse, that is to say, with the exception of his father, who said he was too busy, but felt sure it was nothing serious. ('Why, when I was a boy, my dear, I used to think nothing of an occasional tumble. There's nothing the matter with Dick. Why, etc., etc.')

Trentham's sister was his first visitor.

'I say,' said he, when he had satisfied her on the subject of his health, 'would you like to do me a good turn?'

She intimated that she would be delighted, and asked for details.

'Buy the beak's cat,' hissed Trentham, in a hoarse whisper.

'Dick, it was your leg that you hurt, wasn't it? Not—not your head?' she replied. 'I mean—'

'No, I really mean it. Why can't you? It's a perfectly simple thing to do.'

'But what is a beak? And why should I buy its cat?'

'A beak's a master. Surely you know that. You see, Prater's got a cat lately, and the beast strolls in and raids the studies. Got round over half a pound of prime sausages in here the other night, and he's always bagging things everywhere. You'd be doing everyone a kindness if you would take him on. He'll get lynched some day if you don't. Besides, you want a cat for your new house, surely. Keep down the mice, and that sort of thing, you know. This animal's a demon for mice.' This was a telling argument. Trentham's sister had lately been married, and she certainly had had some idea of investing in a cat to adorn her home. 'As for beetles,' continued the invalid, pushing home his advantage, 'they simply daren't come out of their lairs for fear of him.'

'If he eats beetles,' objected his sister, 'he can't have a very good coat.'

'He doesn't eat them. Just squashes them, you know, like a policeman. He's a decent enough beast as far as looks go.'

'But if he steals things—'

'No, don't you see, he only does that here, because the Praters don't interfere with him and don't let us do anything to him. He won't try that sort of thing on with you. If he does, get somebody to hit him over the head with a boot-jack or something. He'll soon drop it then. You might as well, you know. The House'll simply black your boots if you do.'

'But would Mr. Prater let me have the cat?'

'Try him, anyhow. Pitch it fairly warm, you know. Only cat you ever loved, and that sort of thing.'

'Very well. I'll try.'

'Thanks, awfully. And, I say, you might just look in here on your way out and report.'

Mr.s James Williamson, nee Miss Trentham, made her way dutifully to the Merevale's part of the House. Mr.s Prater had expressed a hope that she would have some tea before catching her train. With tea it is usual to have milk, and with milk it is usual, if there is a cat in the house, to have feline society. Captain Kettle, which was the name thought suitable to this cat by his godfathers and godmothers, was on hand early. As he stood there pawing the mat impatiently, and mewing in a minor key, Mr.s Williamson felt that here was the cat for her. He certainly was good to look upon. His black heart was hidden by a sleek coat of tabby fur, which rendered stroking a luxury. His scheming brain was out of sight in a shapely head.

'Oh, what a lovely cat!' said Mr.s Williamson.

'Yes, isn't he,' agreed Mr.s Prater. 'We are very proud of him.'

'Such a beautiful coat!'

'And such a sweet purr!'

'He looks so intelligent. Has he any tricks?'

Had he any tricks! Why, Mr.s Williamson, he could do everything except speak. Captain Kettle, you bad boy, come here and die for your country. Puss, puss.

Captain Kettle came at last reluctantly, died for his country in record time, and flashed back again to the saucer. He had an important appointment. Sorry to appear rude and all that sort of thing, don't you know, but he had to see a cat about a mouse.

'Well?' said Trentham, when his sister looked in upon him an hour later.

'Oh, Dick, it's the nicest cat I ever saw. I shall never be happy if I don't get it.'

'Have you bought it?' asked the practical Trentham.

'My dear Dick, I couldn't. We couldn't bargain about a cat during tea. Why, I never met Mr.s Prater before this afternoon.'

'No, I suppose not,' admitted Trentham, gloomily. 'Anyhow, look here, if anything turns up to make the beak want to get rid of it, I'll tell him you're dead nuts on it. See?'

For a fortnight after this episode matters went on as before. Mr.s Williamson departed, thinking regretfully of the cat she had left behind her.

Captain Kettle died for his country with moderate regularity, and on one occasion, when he attempted to extract some milk from the very centre of a fag's tea-party, almost died for another reason. Then the end came suddenly.

Trentham had been invited to supper one Sunday by Mr. Prater. When he arrived it became apparent to him that the atmosphere was one of subdued gloom. At first he could not understand this, but soon the reason was made clear. Captain Kettle had, in the expressive language of the man in the street, been and gone and done it. He had been left alone that evening in the drawing-room, while the House was at church, and his eye, roaming restlessly about in search of evil to perform, had lighted upon a cage. In that cage was a special sort of canary, in its own line as accomplished an artiste as Captain Kettle himself. It sang with taste and feeling, and made itself generally agreeable in a number of little ways. But to Captain Kettle it was merely a bird. One of the poets sings of an acquaintance of his who was so constituted that 'a priMr.ose by the river's brim a simple priMr.ose was to him, and it was nothing more'. Just so with Captain Kettle. He was not the cat to make nice distinctions between birds. Like the cat in another poem, he only knew they made him light and salutary meals. So, with the exercise of considerable ingenuity, he extracted that canary from its cage and ate it. He was now in disgrace.

'We shall have to get rid of him,' said Mr. Prater.

'I'm afraid so,' said Mr.s Prater.

'If you weren't thinking of giving him to anyone in particular, sir,' said Trentham, 'my sister would be awfully glad to take him, I know. She was very keen on him when she came to see me.'

'That's excellent,' said Prater. 'I was afraid we should have to send him to a home somewhere.'

'I suppose we can't keep him after all?' suggested Mr.s Prater.

Trentham waited in suspense.

'No,' said Prater, decidedly. 'I think not.' So Captain Kettle went, and the House knew him no more, and the Tabby Terror was at an end.

12

THE PRIZE POEM

Some quarter of a century before the period with which this story deals, a certain rich and misanthropic man was seized with a bright idea for perpetuating his memory after death, and at the same time harassing a certain section of mankind. So in his will he set aside a portion of his income to be spent on an annual prize for the best poem submitted by a member of the Sixth Form of St Austin's College, on a subject to be selected by the Headmaster. And, he added—one seems to hear him chuckling to himself—every member of the form must compete. Then he died. But the evil that men do lives after them, and each year saw a fresh band of unwilling bards goaded to despair by his bequest. True, there were always one or two who hailed this ready market for their sonnets and odes with joy. But the majority, being barely able to rhyme 'dove' with 'love', regarded the annual announcement of the subject chosen with feelings of the deepest disgust.

The chains were thrown off after a period of twenty-seven years in this fashion.

Reynolds of the Remove was indirectly the cause of the change. He was in the infirmary, convalescing after an attack of German measles, when he received a visit from Smith, an ornament of the Sixth.

'By Jove,' remarked that gentleman, gazing enviously round the sick-room, 'they seem to do you pretty well here.'

'Yes, not bad, is it? Take a seat. Anything been happening lately?'

'Nothing much. I suppose you know we beat the M.C.C. by a wicket?'

'Yes, so I heard. Anything else?'

'Prize poem,' said Smith, without enthusiasm. He was not a poet.

Reynolds became interested at once. If there was one role in which he fancied himself (and, indeed, there were a good many), it was that of a versifier. His great ambition was to see some of his lines in print, and he had contracted the habit of sending them up to various periodicals, with no result, so far, except the arrival of rejected MSS. at meal-times in embarrassingly long envelopes. Which he blushingly concealed with all possible speed.

'What's the subject this year?' he asked.

'The College—of all idiotic things.'

'Couldn't have a better subject for an ode. By Jove, I wish I was in the Sixth.'

'Wish I was in the infirmary,' said Smith.

Reynolds was struck with an idea.

'Look here, Smith,' he said, 'if you like I'll do you a poem, and you can send it up. If it gets the prize—'

'Oh, it won't get the prize,' Smith put in eagerly. 'Rogers is a cert. for that.'

'If it gets the prize,' repeated Reynolds, with asperity, 'you'll have to tell the Old Man all about it. He'll probably curse a bit, but that can't be helped. How's this for a beginning?

> *"Imposing pile, reared up 'midst pleasant grounds,*
> *The scene of many a battle, lost or won,*
> *At cricket or at football; whose red walls*
> *Full many a sun has kissed 'ere day is done."'*

'Grand. Couldn't you get in something about the M.C.C. match? You could make cricket rhyme with wicket.' Smith sat entranced with his ingenuity, but the other treated so material a suggestion with scorn.

'Well,' said Smith, 'I must be off now. We've got a House-match on. Thanks awfully about the poem.'

Left to himself, Reynolds set himself seriously to the composing of an ode that should do him justice. That is to say, he drew up a chair and table to the open window, wrote down the lines he had already composed, and began chewing a pen. After a few minutes he wrote another four lines, crossed them out, and selected a fresh piece of paper. He then copied out his first four lines again. After eating his pen to a stump, he jotted down the two words 'boys' and 'joys' at the end of separate lines. This led him to select a third piece of paper, on which he produced a sort of edition de luxe in his best handwriting, with the title 'Ode to the College' in printed letters at the top. He was admiring the neat effect of this when the door opened suddenly and violently, and Mr.s Lee, a lady of advanced years and energetic habits, whose duty it was to minister to the needs of the sick and wounded in the infirmary, entered with his tea. Mr.s Lee's method of entering a room was in accordance with the advice of the Psalmist, where he says, 'Fling wide the gates'. She flung wide the gate of the sick-room, and the result was that what is commonly called 'a thorough draught' was established. The air was

99

thick with flying papers, and when calm at length succeeded storm, two editions of 'Ode to the College' were lying on the grass outside.

Reynolds attacked the tea without attempting to retrieve his vanished work. Poetry is good, but tea is better. Besides, he argued within himself, he remembered all he had written, and could easily write it out again. So, as far as he was concerned, those three sheets of paper were a closed book.

Later on in the afternoon, Montgomery of the Sixth happened to be passing by the infirmary, when Fate, aided by a sudden gust of wind, blew a piece of paper at him. 'Great Scott,' he observed, as his eye fell on the words 'Ode to the College'. Montgomery, like Smith, was no expert in poetry. He had spent a wretched afternoon trying to hammer out something that would pass muster in the poem competition, but without the least success. There were four lines on the paper. Two more, and it would be a poem, and capable of being entered for the prize as such. The words 'imposing pile', with which the fragment in his hand began, took his fancy immensely. A poetic afflatus seized him, and in less than three hours he had added the necessary couplet,

> *How truly sweet it is for such as me*
> *To gaze on thee.*

'And dashed neat, too,' he said, with satisfaction, as he threw the manuscript into his drawer. 'I don't know whether "me" shouldn't be "I", but they'll have to lump it. It's a poem, anyhow, within the meaning of the act.' And he strolled off to a neighbour's study to borrow a book.

Two nights afterwards, Morrison, also of the Sixth, was enjoying his usual during prep siesta in his study. A tap at the door roused him. Hastily seizing a lexicon, he assumed the attitude of the seeker after knowledge, and said, 'Come in.' It was not the House-master, but Evans, Morrison's fag, who entered with pride on his face and a piece of paper in his hand.

'I say,' he began, 'you remember you told me to hunt up some tags for the poem. Will this do?'

Morrison took the paper with a judicial air. On it were the words:

> *Imposing pile, reared up 'midst pleasant grounds,*
> *The scene of many a battle, lost or won,*
> *At cricket or at football; whose red walls*
> *Full many a sun has kissed 'ere day is done.*

'That's ripping, as far as it goes,' said Morrison. 'Couldn't be better. You'll find some apples in that box. Better take a few. But look here,' with sudden suspicion, 'I don't believe you made all this up yourself. Did you?'

Evans finished selecting his apples before venturing on a reply. Then he blushed, as much as a member of the junior school is capable of blushing.

'Well,' he said, 'I didn't exactly. You see, you only told me to get the tags. You didn't say how.'

'But how did you get hold of this? Whose is it?'

'Dunno. I found it in the field between the Pavilion and the infirmary.'

'Oh! well, it doesn't matter much. They're just what I wanted, which is the great thing. Thanks. Shut the door, will you?' Whereupon Evans retired, the richer by many apples, and Morrison resumed his siesta at the point where he had left off.

'Got that poem done yet?' said Smith to Reynolds, pouring out a cup of tea for the invalid on the following Sunday.

'Two lumps, please. No, not quite.'

'Great Caesar, man, when'll it be ready, do you think? It's got to go in tomorrow.'

'Well, I'm really frightfully sorry, but I got hold of a grand book. Ever read—?'

'Isn't any of it done?' asked Smith.

'Only the first verse, I'm afraid. But, look here, you aren't keen on getting the prize. Why not send in only the one verse? It makes a fairly decent poem.'

'Hum! Think the Old 'Un'll pass it?'

'He'll have to. There's nothing in the rules about length. Here it is if you want it.'

'Thanks. I suppose it'll be all right? So long! I must be off.'

The Headmaster, known to the world as the Rev. Arthur James Perceval, M.A., and to the School as the Old 'Un, was sitting at breakfast, stirring his coffee, with a look of marked perplexity upon his dignified face. This was not caused by the coffee, which was excellent, but by a letter which he held in his left hand.

'Hum!' he said. Then 'Umph!' in a protesting tone, as if someone had pinched him. Finally, he gave vent to a long-drawn 'Um-m-m,' in a deep bass. 'Most extraordinary. Really, most extraordinary. Exceedingly. Yes. Um. Very.' He took a sip of coffee.

'My dear,' said he, suddenly. Mr.s Perceval started violently. She had been sketching out in her mind a little dinner, and wondering whether the cook would be equal to it.

101

'Yes,' she said.

'My dear, this is a very extraordinary communication. Exceedingly so. Yes, very.'

'Who is it from?'

Mr. Perceval shuddered. He was a purist in speech. 'From whom, you should say. It is from Mr. Wells, a great College friend of mine. I—ah—submitted to him for examination the poems sent in for the Sixth Form Prize. He writes in a very flippant style. I must say, very flippant. This is his letter:—"Dear Jimmy (really, really, he should remember that we are not so young as we were); dear—ahem—Jimmy. The poems to hand. I have read them, and am writing this from my sick-bed. The doctor tells me I may pull through even yet. There was only one any good at all, that was Rogers's, which, though—er—squiffy (tut!) in parts, was a long way better than any of the others. But the most taking part of the whole programme was afforded by the three comedians, whose efforts I enclose. You will notice that each begins with exactly the same four lines. Of course, I deprecate cribbing, but you really can't help admiring this sort of thing. There is a reckless daring about it which is simply fascinating. A horrible thought—have they been pulling your dignified leg? By the way, do you remember"—the rest of the letter is—er—on different matters.'

'James! How extraordinary!'

'Um, yes. I am reluctant to suspect—er—collusion, but really here there can be no doubt. No doubt at all. No.'

'Unless,' began Mr.s Perceval, tentatively. 'No doubt at all, my dear,' snapped Reverend Jimmy. He did not wish to recall the other possibility, that his dignified leg was being pulled.

'Now, for what purpose did I summon you three boys?' asked Mr. Perceval, of Smith, Montgomery, and Morrison, in his room after morning school that day. He generally began a painful interview with this question. The method had distinct advantages. If the criminal were of a nervous disposition, he would give himself away upon the instant. In any case, it was likely to startle him. 'For what purpose?' repeated the Headmaster, fixing Smith with a glittering eye.

'I will tell you,' continued Mr. Perceval. 'It was because I desired information, which none but you can supply. How comes it that each of your compositions for the Poetry Prize commences with the same four lines?' The three poets looked at one another in speechless astonishment.

'Here,' he resumed, 'are the three papers. Compare them. Now,'—after the inspection was over—' what explanation have you to offer? Smith, are these your lines?'

102

'I—er—ah—wrote them, sir.'

'Don't prevaricate, Smith. Are you the author of those lines?'

'No, sir.'

'Ah! Very good. Are you, Montgomery?'

'No, sir.'

'Very good. Then you, Morrison, are exonerated from all blame. You have been exceedingly badly treated. The first-fruit of your brain has been—ah—plucked by others, who toiled not neither did they spin. You can go, Morrison.'

'But, sir—'

'Well, Morrison?'

'I didn't write them, sir.'

'I—ah—don't quite understand you, Morrison. You say that you are indebted to another for these lines?'

'Yes, sir.'

'To Smith?'

'No, sir.'

'To Montgomery?'

'No, sir.'

'Then, Morrison, may I ask to whom you are indebted?'

'I found them in the field on a piece of paper, sir.' He claimed the discovery himself, because he thought that Evans might possibly prefer to remain outside this tangle.

'So did I, sir.' This from Montgomery. Mr. Perceval looked bewildered, as indeed he was.

'And did you, Smith, also find this poem on a piece of paper in the field?' There was a metallic ring of sarcasm in his voice.

'No, sir.'

'Ah! Then to what circumstance were you indebted for the lines?'

'I got Reynolds to do them for me, sir.'

Montgomery spoke. 'It was near the infirmary that I found the paper, and Reynolds is in there.'

'So did I, sir,' said Morrison, incoherently.

'Then am I to understand, Smith, that to gain the prize you resorted to such underhand means as this?'

'No, sir, we agreed that there was no danger of my getting the prize. If I had got it, I should have told you everything. Reynolds will tell you that, sir.'

'Then what object had you in pursuing this deception?'

'Well, sir, the rules say everyone must send in something, and I can't write poetry at all, and Reynolds likes it, so I asked him to do it.'

And Smith waited for the storm to burst. But it did not burst. Far down in Mr. Perceval's system lurked a quiet sense of humour. The situation penetrated to it. Then he remembered the examiner's letter, and it dawned upon him that there are few crueller things than to make a prosaic person write poetry.

'You may go,' he said, and the three went.

And at the next Board Meeting it was decided, mainly owing to the influence of an exceedingly eloquent speech from the Headmaster, to alter the rules for the Sixth Form Poetry Prize, so that from thence onward no one need compete unless he felt himself filled with the immortal fire.

13

WORK

With a pleasure that's emphatic
We retire to our attic
With the satisfying feeling that our duty has been done.

Oh! philosophers may sing
Of the troubles of a king
But of pleasures there are many and of troubles there are none,
And the culminating pleasure
Which we treasure beyond measure
Is the satisfying feeling that our duty has been done.

W. S. Gilbert

Work is supposed to be the centre round which school life revolves—the hub of the school wheel, the lode-star of the schoolboy's existence, and a great many other things. 'You come to school to work', is the formula used by masters when sentencing a victim to the wailing and gnashing of teeth provided by two hours' extra tuition on a hot afternoon. In this, I think, they err, and my opinion is backed up by numerous scholars of my acquaintance, who have even gone so far—on occasions when they themselves have been the victims—as to express positive disapproval of the existing state of things. In the dear, dead days (beyond recall), I used often to long to put the case to my form-master in its only fair aspect, but always refrained from motives of policy. Masters are so apt to take offence at the well-meant endeavours of their form to instruct them in the way they should go.

What I should have liked to have done would have been something after this fashion. Entering the sanctum of the Headmaster, I should have motioned him to his seat—if he were seated already, have assured him that to rise was unnecessary. I should then have taken a seat myself, taking care to preserve a calm fixity of demeanour, and finally, with a preliminary cough, I should have embarked upon the following moving address: 'My dear sir, my dear Reverend Jones or Brown (as the case may be), believe me when I say that your whole system of work is founded on a fallacious dream and reeks of rottenness. No, no, I beg that you will not interrupt me. The real state of the case, if I may say so, is briefly this: a boy goes to school to enjoy himself, and, on arriving, finds to his consternation that a great deal more work is expected of him than he is prepared to do. What course, then, Reverend Jones or Brown, does he take? He proceeds to do as much work as will steer him safely between the, ah—I may say, the Scylla of punishment and the Charybdis of being considered what my, er—fellow-pupils euphoniously term a swot. That, I think, is all this morning. Good day. Pray do not trouble to rise. I will find my way out.' I should then have made for the door, locked it, if possible, on the outside, and, rushing to the railway station, have taken a through ticket to Spitzbergen or some other place where Extradition treaties do not hold good.

But 'twas not mine to play the Tib. Gracchus, to emulate the O. Cromwell. So far from pouring my opinions like so much boiling oil into the ear of my task-master, I was content to play the part of audience while he did the talking, my sole remark being 'Yes'r' at fixed intervals.

And yet I knew that I was in the right. My bosom throbbed with the justice of my cause. For why? The ambition of every human new boy is surely to become like J. Essop of the First Eleven, who can hit a ball over two ponds, a wood, and seven villages, rather than to resemble that pale young student, Mill-Stuart, who, though he can speak Sanskrit like a native of Sanskritia, couldn't score a single off a slow long-hop.

And this ambition is a laudable one. For the athlete is the product of nature—a step towards the more perfect type of animal, while the scholar is the outcome of artificiality. What, I ask, does the scholar gain, either morally or physically, or in any other way, by knowing who was tribune of the people in 284 BC or what is the precise difference between the various constructions of cum? It is not as if ignorance of the tribune's identity caused him any mental unrest. In short, what excuse is there for the student? 'None,' shrieks Echo enthusiastically. 'None whatever.'

Our children are being led to ruin by this system. They will become dons and think in Greek. The victim of the craze stops at nothing. He puns in Latin. He quips and quirks in Ionic and Doric. In the worst stages of the disease he will edit Greek plays and say that Merry quite misses the fun of the passage, or that Jebb is mediocre. Think, I beg of you, paterfamilias, and you, mater ditto, what your feelings would be were you to find Henry or Archibald Cuthbert correcting proofs of The Agamemnon, and inventing 'nasty ones' for Mr. Sidgwick! Very well then. Be warned.

Our bright-eyed lads are taught insane constructions in Greek and Latin from morning till night, and they come for their holidays, in many cases, without the merest foundation of a batting style. Ask them what a Yorker is, and they will say: 'A man from York, though I presume you mean a Yorkshireman.' They will read Herodotus without a dictionary for pleasure, but ask them to translate the childishly simple sentence: 'Trott was soon in his timber-yard with a length 'un that whipped across from the off,' and they'll shrink abashed and swear they have not skill at that, as Gilbert says.

The papers sometimes contain humorous forecasts of future education, when cricket and football shall come to their own. They little know the excellence of the thing they mock at. When we get schools that teach nothing but games, then will the sun definitely refuse to set on the roast beef of old England. May it be soon. Some day, mayhap, I shall gather my great-great-grandsons round my knee, and tell them—as one tells tales of Faery—that I can remember the time when Work was considered the be-all and the end-all of a school career. Perchance, when my great-great-grandson John (called John after the famous Jones of that name) has brought home the prize for English Essay on 'Rugby v. Association', I shall pat his head (gently) and the tears will come to my old eyes as I recall the time when I, too, might have won a prize—for that obsolete subject, Latin Prose—and was only prevented by the superior excellence of my thirty-and-one fellow students, coupled, indeed, with my own inability to conjugate sum.

Such days, I say, may come. But now are the Dark Ages. The only thing that can possibly make Work anything but an unmitigated nuisance is the prospect of a 'Varsity scholarship, and the thought that, in the event of failure, a 'Varsity career will be out of the question.

With this thought constantly before him, the student can put a certain amount of enthusiasm into his work, and even go to the length of rising at five o'clock o' mornings to drink yet deeper of the cup of knowledge. I have done it myself. 'Varsity means games and yellow waistcoats and Proctors, and that sort of thing. It is worth working for.

But for the unfortunate individual who is barred by circumstances from participating in these joys, what inducement is there to work? Is such a one to leave the school nets in order to stew in a stuffy room over a Thucydides? I trow not.

Chapter one of my great forthcoming work, The Compleat Slacker, contains minute instructions on the art of avoiding preparation from beginning to end of term. Foremost among the words of advice ranks this maxim: Get an official list of the books you are to do, and examine them carefully with a view to seeing what it is possible to do unseen. Thus, if Virgil is among these authors, you can rely on being able to do him with success. People who ought to know better will tell you that Virgil is hard. Such a shallow falsehood needs little comment. A scholar who cannot translate ten lines of The Aeneid between the time he is put on and the time he begins to speak is unworthy of pity or consideration, and if I meet him in the street I shall assuredly cut him. Aeschylus, on the other hand, is a demon, and needs careful watching, though in an emergency you can always say the reading is wrong.

Sometimes the compleat slacker falls into a trap. The saddest case I can remember is that of poor Charles Vanderpoop. He was a bright young lad, and showed some promise of rising to heights as a slacker. He fell in this fashion. One Easter term his form had half-finished a speech of Demosthenes, and the form-master gave them to understand that they would absorb the rest during the forthcoming term. Charles, being naturally anxious to do as little work as possible during the summer months, spent his Easter holidays carefully preparing this speech, so as to have it ready in advance. What was his horror, on returning to School at the appointed date, to find that they were going to throw Demosthenes over altogether, and patronize Plato. Threats, entreaties, prayers—all were accounted nothing by the master who had led him into this morass of troubles. It is believed that the shock destroyed his reason. At any rate, the fact remains that that term (the summer term, mark you) he won two prizes. In the following term he won three. To recapitulate his outrages from that time to the present were a harrowing and unnecessary task. Suffice it that he is now a Regius Professor, and I saw in the papers a short time ago that a lecture of his on 'The Probable Origin of the Greek Negative', created quite a furore. If this is not Tragedy with a big T, I should like to know what it is.

As an exciting pastime, unseen translation must rank very high. Everyone who has ever tried translating unseen must acknowledge that all other forms of excitement seem but feeble makeshifts after it. I have, in the course of a career of sustained usefulness to the human race, had my share of thrills. I have asked a strong and busy porter, at Paddington, when the Brighton train started. I have gone for the broad-jump record in trying to avoid a motor-car. I have played Spillikins and Ping-Pong. But never again have I felt the excitement that used to wander athwart my moral backbone when I was put on to translate a passage containing a notorious crux and seventeen doubtful readings, with only that innate genius, which is the wonder of the civilized world, to pull me through. And what a glow of pride one feels when it is all over; when one has made a glorious, golden guess at the crux, and trampled the doubtful readings under foot with inspired ease. It is like a day at the seaside.

Work is bad enough, but Examinations are worse, especially the Board Examinations. By doing from ten to twenty minutes prep every night, the compleat slacker could get through most of the term with average success. Then came the Examinations. The dabbler in unseen translations found himself caught as in a snare. Gone was the peaceful security in which he had lulled to rest all the well-meant efforts of his guardian angel to rouse him to a sense of his duties. There, right in front of him, yawned the abyss of Retribution.

Alas! poor slacker. I knew him, Horatio; a fellow of infinite jest, of most excellent fancy. Where be his gibes now? How is he to cope with the fiendish ingenuity of the examiners? How is he to master the contents of a book of Thucydides in a couple of days? It is a fearsome problem. Perhaps he will get up in the small hours and work by candle light from two till eight o'clock. In this case he will start his day a mental and physical wreck. Perhaps he will try to work and be led away by the love of light reading.

In any case he will fail to obtain enough marks to satisfy the examiners, though whether examiners ever are satisfied, except by Harry the hero of the school story (Every Lad's Library, uniform edition, 2s 6d), is rather a doubtful question.

In such straits, matters resolve themselves into a sort of drama with three characters. We will call our hero Smith.

Scene: a Study

> *Dramatis Personae:*
> *SMITH*
> *CONSCIENCE*
> *MEPHISTOPHELES*

Enter SMITH (*down centre*)
He seats himself at table and opens a Thucydides.
Enter   CONSCIENCE   *through*   *ceiling*   (*R.*), MEPHISTOPHELES *through floor* (*L.*).

CONSCIENCE (*with a kindly smile*): *Precisely what I was about to remark, my dear lad. A little Thucydides would be a very good thing. Thucydides, as you doubtless know, was a very famous Athenian historian. Date?*

SMITH: *Er—um—let me see.*

MEPH. *(aside): Look in the Introduction and pretend you did it by accident.*

SMITH *(having done so):* 431 B.C. circ.

CONSCIENCE *wipes away a tear.*

CONSCIENCE: *Thucydides made himself a thorough master of the concisest of styles.*

MEPH.: *And in doing so became infernally obscure. Excuse shop.*

SMITH *(gloomily):* Hum!

MEPH. *(sneeringly): Ha!*

Long pause.

CONSCIENCE *(gently):* Do you not think, my dear lad, that you had better begin? Time and tide, as you are aware, wait for no man. And—

SMITH: Yes?

CONSCIENCE: You have not, I fear, a very firm grasp of the subject. However, if you work hard till eleven—

SMITH *(gloomily):* Hum! Three hours!

MEPH. *(cheerily):* Exactly so. Three hours. A little more if anything. By the way, excuse me asking, but have you prepared the subject thoroughly during the term?

SMITH: My dear sir! Of course!

CONSCIENCE *(reprovingly)*:???!!??!

SMITH: Well, perhaps, not quite so much as I might have done. Such a lot of things to do this term. Cricket, for instance.

MEPH.: Rather. Talking of cricket, you seemed to be shaping rather well last Saturday. I had just run up on business, and someone told me you made eighty not out. Get your century all right?

SMITH *(brightening at the recollection):* Just a bit—117 not out. I hit—but perhaps you've heard?

MEPH.: Not at all, not at all. Let's hear all about it.

CONSCIENCE *seeks to interpose, but is prevented by MEPH., who eggs SMITH on to talk cricket for over an hour.*

CONSCIENCE *(at last; in an acid voice):* That is a history of the Peloponnesian War by Thucydides on the table in front of you. I thought I would mention it, in case you had forgotten.

SMITH: Great Scott, yes! Here, I say, I must start.

CONSCIENCE: Hear! Hear!

MEPH. *(insinuatingly):* One moment. Did you say you had prepared this book during the term? Afraid I'm a little hard of hearing. Eh, what?

SMITH: Well—er—no, I have not. Have you ever played billiards with a walking-stick and five balls?

MEPH.: Quite so, quite so. I quite understand. Don't you distress yourself, old chap. You obviously can't get through a whole book of Thucydides in under two hours, can you?

CONSCIENCE (*severely*): He might, by attentive application to study, master a considerable portion of the historian's chef d'oeuvre in that time.

MEPH.: Yes, and find that not one of the passages he had prepared was set in the paper.

CONSCIENCE: At the least, he would, if he were to pursue the course which I have indicated, greatly benefit his mind.

MEPH. gives a short, derisive laugh. Long pause.

MEPH. (*looking towards bookshelf*): Hullo, you've got a decent lot of books, pommy word you have. Rodney Stone, Vice Versa, Many Cargoes. Ripping. Ever read Many Cargoes?

CONSCIENCE (*glancing at his watch*): I am sorry, but I must really go now. I will see you some other day.

Exit sorrowfully.

MEPH.: Well, thank goodness he's gone. Never saw such a fearful old bore in my life. Can't think why you let him hang on to you so. We may as well make a night of it now, eh? No use your trying to work at this time of night.

SMITH: Not a bit.

MEPH.: Did you say you'd not read Many Cargoes?

SMITH: Never. Only got it today. Good?

MEPH.: Simply ripping. All short stories. Make you yell.

SMITH (*with a last effort*): But don't you think—

MEPH.: Oh no. Besides, you can easily get up early tomorrow for the Thucydides.

SMITH: Of course I can. Never thought of that. Heave us Many Cargoes. Thanks.

Begins to read. MEPH. grins fiendishly, and vanishes through floor enveloped in red flame. Sobbing heard from the direction of the ceiling.

Scene closes.

Next morning, of course, he will oversleep himself, and his Thucydides paper will be of such a calibre that that eminent historian will writhe in his grave.

14

NOTES

Of all forms of lettered effusiveness, that which exploits the original work of others and professes to supply us with right opinions thereanent is the least wanted.

Kenneth Grahame

It has always seemed to me one of the worst flaws in our mistaken social system, that absolutely no distinction is made between the master who forces the human boy to take down notes from dictation and the rest of mankind. I mean that, if in a moment of righteous indignation you rend such a one limb from limb, you will almost certainly be subjected to the utmost rigour of the law, and you will be lucky if you escape a heavy fine of five or ten shillings, exclusive of the costs of the case. Now, this is not right on the face of it. It is even wrong. The law should take into account the extreme provocation which led to the action. Punish if you will the man who travels second-class with a third-class ticket, or who borrows a pencil and forgets to return it; but there are occasions when justice should be tempered with mercy, and this murdering of pedagogues is undoubtedly such an occasion.

It should be remembered, however, that there are two varieties of notes. The printed notes at the end of your Thucydides or Homer are distinctly useful when they aim at acting up to their true vocation, namely, the translating of difficult passages or words. Sometimes, however, the author will insist on airing his scholarship, and instead of translations he supplies parallel passages, which neither interest, elevate, nor amuse the reader. This, of course, is mere vanity. The author, sitting in his comfortable chair with something short within easy reach, recks nothing of the misery he is inflicting on hundreds of people who have done him no harm at all. He turns over the pages of his book of Familiar Quotations with brutal callousness, and for every tricky passage in the work which he is editing, finds and makes a note of three or four even trickier ones from other works. Who has not in his time been brought face to face with a word which defies translation? There are two courses open to you on such an occasion, to look the word up in the lexicon, or in the notes. You, of course, turn up the notes, and find: 'See line

112

80.' You look up line 80, hoping to see a translation, and there you are told that a rather similar construction occurs in Xenophades' Lyrics from a Padded Cell. On this, the craven of spirit will resort to the lexicon, but the man of mettle will close his book with an emphatic bang, and refuse to have anything more to do with it. Of a different sort are the notes which simply translate the difficulty and subside. These are a boon to the scholar. Without them it would be almost impossible to prepare one's work during school, and we should be reduced to the prosaic expedient of working in prep. time. What we want is the commentator who translates mensa as 'a table' without giving a page and a half of notes on the uses of the table in ancient Greece, with an excursus on the habit common in those times of retiring underneath it after dinner, and a list of the passages in Apollonius Rhodius where the word 'table' is mentioned.

These voluminous notes are apt to prove a nuisance in more ways than one. Your average master is generally inordinately fond of them, and will frequently ask some member of the form to read his note on so-and-so out to his fellows. This sometimes leads to curious results, as it is hardly to be expected that the youth called upon will be attending, even if he is awake, which is unlikely. On one occasion an acquaintance of mine, 'whose name I am not at liberty to divulge', was suddenly aware that he was being addressed, and, on giving the matter his attention, found that it was the form-master asking him to read out his note on Balbus murum aedificavit. My friend is a kind-hearted youth and of an obliging disposition, and would willingly have done what was asked of him, but there were obstacles, first and foremost of which ranked the fact that, taking advantage of his position on the back desk (whither he thought the basilisk eye of Authority could not reach), he had substituted Bab Ballads for the words of Virgil, and was engrossed in the contents of that modern classic. The subsequent explanations lasted several hours. In fact, it is probable that the master does not understand the facts of the case thoroughly even now. It is true that he called him a 'loathsome, slimy, repulsive toad', but even this seems to fall short of the grandeur of the situation.

Those notes, also, which are, alas! only too common nowadays, that deal with peculiarities of grammar, how supremely repulsive they are! It is impossible to glean any sense from them, as the Editor mixes up Nipperwick's view with Sidgeley's reasoning and Spreckendzedeutscheim's surmise with Donnerundblitzendorf's conjecture in a way that seems to argue a thorough unsoundness of mind and morals, a cynical insanity combined with a blatant indecency. He occasionally starts in a reasonable manner by giving one view as (1) and the next as (2). So far everyone is happy and satisfied. The trouble commences when he has occasion to refer back to some former view, when he will say: 'Thus we see (1) and (14) that,' etc. The unlucky student puts a finger on the page to keep the place, and hunts up view one. Having found this, and marked the spot with another finger, he proceeds to look up view fourteen. He places another finger on this, and reads on, as follows: 'Zmpe, however, maintains that Schrumpff (see 3) is practically insane, that Spleckzh (see 34) is only a little better, and that Rswkg (see 97 a (b) C3) is so far from being right that his views may be dismissed as readily as those of Xkryt (see 5x).' At this point brain-fever sets in, the victim's last coherent thought being a passionate wish for more fingers. A friend of mine who was the wonder of all who knew him, in that he was known to have scored ten per cent in one of these papers on questions like the above, once divulged to an interviewer the fact that he owed his success to his methods of learning rather than to his ability. On the night before an exam, he would retire to some secret, solitary place, such as the boot-room, and commence learning these notes by heart. This, though a formidable task, was not so bad as the other alternative. The result was that, although in the majority of cases he would put down for one question an answer that would have been right for another, yet occasionally, luck being with him, he would hit the mark. Hence his ten per cent.

Another fruitful source of discomfort is provided by the type of master who lectures on a subject for half an hour, and then, with a bland smile, invites, or rather challenges, his form to write a 'good, long note' on the quintessence of his discourse. For the inexperienced this is an awful moment. They must write something—but what? For the last half hour they have been trying to impress the master with the fact that they belong to the class of people who can always listen best with their eyes closed. Nor poppy, nor mandragora, nor all the drowsy syrups of the world can ever medicine them to that sweet sleep that they have just been enjoying. And now they must write a 'good, long note'. It is in such extremities that your veteran shows up well. He does not betray any discomfort. Not he. He rather enjoys the prospect, in fact, of being permitted to place the master's golden eloquence on paper. So he takes up his pen with alacrity. No need to think what to write. He embarks on an essay concerning the master, showing up all his flaws in a pitiless light, and analysing his thorough worthlessness of character. On so congenial a subject he can, of course, write reams, and as the master seldom, if ever, desires to read the 'good, long note', he acquires a well-earned reputation for attending in school and being able to express himself readily with his pen. Vivat floreatque.

But all these forms of notes are as nothing compared with the notes that youths even in this our boasted land of freedom are forced to take down from dictation. Of the 'good, long note' your French scholar might well remark: 'C'est terrible', but justice would compel him to add, as he thought of the dictation note: 'mais ce n'est pas le diable'. For these notes from dictation are, especially on a warm day, indubitably le diable.

Such notes are always dictated so rapidly that it is impossible to do anything towards understanding them as you go. You have to write your hardest to keep up. The beauty of this, from one point of view, is that, if you miss a sentence, you have lost the thread of the whole thing, and it is useless to attempt to take it up again at once. The only plan is to wait for some perceptible break in the flow of words, and dash in like lightning. It is much the same sort of thing as boarding a bus when in motion. And so you can take a long rest, provided you are in an obscure part of the room. In passing, I might add that a very pleasing indoor game can be played by asking the master, 'what came after so-and-so?' mentioning a point of the oration some half-hour back. This always provides a respite of a few minutes while he is thinking of some bitter repartee worthy of the occasion, and if repeated several times during an afternoon may cause much innocent merriment.

Of course, the real venom that lurks hid within notes from dictation does not appear until the time for examination arrives. Then you find yourself face to face with sixty or seventy closely and badly written pages of a note-book, all of which must be learnt by heart if you would aspire to the dizzy heights of half-marks. It is useless to tell your examiner that you had no chance of getting up the subject. 'Why,' he will reply, 'I gave you notes on that very thing myself.' 'You did, sir,' you say, as you advance stealthily upon him, 'but as you dictated those notes at the rate of two hundred words a minute, and as my brain, though large, is not capable of absorbing sixty pages of a note-book in one night, how the suggestively asterisked aposiopesis do you expect me to know them? Ah-h-h!' The last word is a war-cry, as you fling yourself bodily on him, and tear him courteously, but firmly, into minute fragments. Experience, which, as we all know, teaches, will in time lead you into adopting some method by which you may evade this taking of notes. A good plan is to occupy yourself with the composition of a journal, an unofficial magazine not intended for the eyes of the profane, but confined rigidly to your own circle of acquaintances.

The chief advantage of such a work is that you will continue to write while the notes are being dictated. To throw your pen down with an air of finality and begin reading some congenial work of fiction would be a gallant action, but impolitic. No, writing of some sort is essential, and as it is out of the question to take down the notes, what better substitute than an unofficial journal could be found? To one whose contributions to the School magazine are constantly being cut down to mere skeletons by the hands of censors, there is a rapture otherwise unattainable in a page of really scurrilous items about those in authority. Try it yourselves, my beamish lads. Think of something really bad about somebody. Write it down and gloat over it. Sometimes, indeed, it is of the utmost use in determining your future career. You will probably remember those Titanic articles that appeared at the beginning of the war in The Weekly Luggage-Train, dealing with all the crimes of the War Office—the generals, the soldiers, the enemy—of everybody, in fact, except the editor, staff and office-boy of The W.L.T. Well, the writer of those epoch-making articles confesses that he owes all his skill to his early training, when, a happy lad at his little desk in school, he used to write trenchantly in his note-book on the subject of the authorities. There is an example for you. Of course we can never be like him, but let, oh! let us be as like him as we're able to be. A final word to those lost ones who dictate the notes. Why are our ears so constantly assailed with unnecessary explanations of, and opinions on, English literature? Prey upon the Classics if you will. It is a revolting habit, but too common to excite overmuch horror. But surely anybody, presupposing a certain bias towards sanity, can understand the Classics of our own language, with the exception, of course, of Browning. Take Tennyson, for example. How often have we been forced to take down from dictation the miserable maunderings of some commentator on the subject of Maud. A person reads Maud, and either likes it or dislikes it. In any case his opinion is not likely to be influenced by writing down at express speed the opinions of somebody else concerning the methods or objectivity and subjectivity of the author when he produced the work.

Somebody told me a short time ago that Shelley was an example of supreme, divine, superhuman genius. It is the sort of thing Mr. Gilbert's 'rapturous maidens' might have said: 'How Botticellian! How Fra Angelican! How perceptively intense and consummately utter!' There is really no material difference.

15

NOW, TALKING ABOUT CRICKET

In the days of yore, when these white hairs were brown—or was it black? At any rate, they were not white—and I was at school, it was always my custom, when Fate obliged me to walk to school with a casual acquaintance, to whom I could not unburden my soul of those profound thoughts which even then occupied my mind, to turn the struggling conversation to the relative merits of cricket and football.

'Do you like cricket better than footer?' was my formula. Now, though at the time, in order to save fruitless argument, I always agreed with my companion, and praised the game he praised, in the innermost depths of my sub-consciousness, cricket ranked a long way in front of all other forms of sport. I may be wrong. More than once in my career it has been represented to me that I couldn't play cricket for nuts. My captain said as much when I ran him out in the match of the season after he had made forty-nine and looked like stopping. A bowling acquaintance heartily endorsed his opinion on the occasion of my missing three catches off him in one over. This, however, I attribute to prejudice, for the man I missed ultimately reached his century, mainly off the deliveries of my bowling acquaintance. I pointed out to him that, had I accepted any one of the three chances, we should have missed seeing the prettiest century made on the ground that season; but he was one of those bowlers who sacrifice all that is beautiful in the game to mere wickets. A sordid practice.

Later on, the persistence with which my county ignored my claims to inclusion in the team, convinced me that I must leave cricket fame to others. True, I did figure, rather prominently, too, in one county match. It was at the Oval, Surrey v. Middlesex. How well I remember that occasion! Albert Trott was bowling (Bertie we used to call him); I forget who was batting. Suddenly the ball came soaring in my direction. I was not nervous. I put down the sandwich I was eating, rose from my seat, picked the ball up neatly, and returned it with unerring aim to a fieldsman who was waiting for it with becoming deference. Thunders of applause went up from the crowded ring.

That was the highest point I ever reached in practical cricket.

But, as the historian says of Mr. Winkle, a man may be an excellent sportsman in theory, even if he fail in practice. That's me. Reader (if any), have you ever played cricket in the passage outside your study with a walking-stick and a ball of paper? That's the game, my boy, for testing your skill of wrist and eye. A century v. the M.C.C. is well enough in its way, but give me the man who can watch 'em in a narrow passage, lit only by a flickering gas-jet—one for every hit, four if it reaches the end, and six if it goes downstairs full-pitch, any pace bowling allowed. To make double figures in such a match is to taste life. Only you had better do your tasting when the House-master is out for the evening.

I like to watch the young cricket idea shooting. I refer to the lower games, where 'next man in' umpires with his pads on, his loins girt, and a bat in his hand. Many people have wondered why it is that no budding umpire can officiate unless he holds a bat. For my part, I think there is little foundation for the theory that it is part of a semi-religious rite, on the analogy of the Freemasons' special handshake and the like. Nor do I altogether agree with the authorities who allege that man, when standing up, needs something as a prop or support. There is a shadow of reason, I grant, in this supposition, but after years of keen observation I am inclined to think that the umpire keeps his bat by him, firstly, in order that no unlicensed hand shall commandeer it unbeknownst, and secondly, so that he shall be ready to go in directly his predecessor is out. There is an ill-concealed restiveness about his movements, as he watches the batsmen getting set, that betrays an overwrought spirit. Then of a sudden one of them plays a ball on to his pad. "s that?' asks the bowler, with an overdone carelessness. 'Clean out. Now I'm in,' and already he is rushing up the middle of the pitch to take possession. When he gets to the wicket a short argument ensues. 'Look here, you idiot, I hit it hard.' 'Rot, man, out of the way.' '!!??!' 'Look here, Smith, are you going to dispute the umpire's decision?' Chorus of fieldsmen: 'Get out, Smith, you ass. You've been given out years ago.' Overwhelmed by popular execration, Smith reluctantly departs, registering in the black depths of his soul a resolution to take on the umpireship at once, with a view to gaining an artistic revenge by giving his enemy run out on the earliest possible occasion. There is a primeval insouciance about this sort of thing which is as refreshing to a mind jaded with the stiff formality of professional umpires as a cold shower-bath.

I have made a special study of last-wicket men; they are divided into two classes, the deplorably nervous, or the outrageously confident. The nervous largely outnumber the confident. The launching of a last-wicket man, when there are ten to make to win, or five minutes left to make a draw of a losing game, is fully as impressive a ceremony as the launching of the latest battleship. An interested crowd harasses the poor victim as he is putting on his pads. 'Feel in a funk?' asks some tactless friend. 'N-n-no, norrabit.' 'That's right,' says the captain encouragingly, 'bowling's as easy as anything.'

This cheers the wretch up a little, until he remembers suddenly that the captain himself was distinctly at sea with the despised trundling, and succumbed to his second ball, about which he obviously had no idea whatever. At this he breaks down utterly, and, if emotional, will sob into his batting glove. He is assisted down the Pavilion steps, and reaches the wickets in a state of collapse. Here, very probably, a reaction will set in. The sight of the crease often comes as a positive relief after the vague terrors experienced in the Pavilion.

The confident last-wicket man, on the other hand, goes forth to battle with a light quip upon his lips. The lot of a last-wicket batsman, with a good eye and a sense of humour, is a very enviable one. The incredulous disgust of the fast bowler, who thinks that at last he may safely try that slow head-ball of his, and finds it lifted genially over the leg-boundary, is well worth seeing. I remember in one school match, the last man, unfortunately on the opposite side, did this three times in one over, ultimately retiring to a fluky catch in the slips with forty-one to his name. Nervousness at cricket is a curious thing. As the author of Willow the King, himself a county cricketer, has said, it is not the fear of getting out that causes funk. It is a sort of intangible je ne sais quoi. I trust I make myself clear. Some batsmen are nervous all through a long innings. With others the feeling disappears with the first boundary.

A young lady—it is, of course, not polite to mention her age to the minute, but it ranged somewhere between eight and ten—was taken to see a cricket match once. After watching the game with interest for some time, she gave out this profound truth: 'They all attend specially to one man.' It would be difficult to sum up the causes of funk more lucidly and concisely. To be an object of interest is sometimes pleasant, but when ten fieldsmen, a bowler, two umpires, and countless spectators are eagerly watching your every movement, the thing becomes embarrassing.

That is why it is, on the whole, preferable to be a cricket spectator rather than a cricket player. No game affords the spectator such unique opportunities of exerting his critical talents. You may have noticed that it is always the reporter who knows most about the game. Everyone, moreover, is at heart a critic, whether he represent the majesty of the Press or not. From the lady of Hoxton, who crushes her friend's latest confection with the words, 'My, wot an 'at!' down to that lowest class of all, the persons who call your attention (in print) to the sinister meaning of everything Clytemnestra says in The Agamemnon, the whole world enjoys expressing an opinion of its own about something.

In football you are vouchsafed fewer chances. Practically all you can do is to shout 'off-side' whenever an opponent scores, which affords but meagre employment for a really critical mind. In cricket, however, nothing can escape you. Everything must be done in full sight of everybody. There the players stand, without refuge, simply inviting criticism.

It is best, however, not to make one's remarks too loud. If you do, you call down upon yourself the attention of others, and are yourself criticized. I remember once, when I was of tender years, watching a school match, and one of the batsmen lifted a ball clean over the Pavilion. This was too much for my sensitive and critical young mind. 'On the carpet, sir,' I shouted sternly, well up in the treble clef, 'keep 'em on the carpet.' I will draw a veil. Suffice it to say that I became a sport and derision, and was careful for the future to criticize in a whisper. But the reverse by no means crushed me. Even now I take a melancholy pleasure in watching school matches, and saying So-and-So will make quite a fair school-boy bat in time, but he must get rid of that stroke of his on the off, and that shocking leg-hit, and a few of those awful strokes in the slips, but that on the whole, he is by no means lacking in promise. I find it refreshing. If, however, you feel compelled not merely to look on, but to play, as one often does at schools where cricket is compulsory, it is impossible to exaggerate the importance of white boots. The game you play before you get white boots is not cricket, but a weak imitation. The process of initiation is generally this. One plays in shoes for a few years with the most dire result, running away to square leg from fast balls, and so on, till despair seizes the soul. Then an angel in human form, in the very effective disguise of the man at the school boot-shop, hints that, for an absurdly small sum in cash, you may become the sole managing director of a pair of white buckskin boots with real spikes. You try them on. They fit, and the initiation is complete. You no longer run away from fast balls. You turn them neatly off to the boundary. In a word, you begin for the first time to play the game, the whole game, and nothing but the game.

There are misguided people who complain that cricket is becoming a business more than a game, as if that were not the most fortunate thing that could happen. When it ceases to be a mere business and becomes a religious ceremony, it will be a sign that the millennium is at hand. The person who regards cricket as anything less than a business is no fit companion, gentle reader, for the likes of you and me. As long as the game goes in his favour the cloven hoof may not show itself. But give him a good steady spell of leather-hunting, and you will know him for what he is, a mere dilettante, a dabbler, in a word, a worm, who ought never to be allowed to play at all. The worst of this species will sometimes take advantage of the fact that the game in which they happen to be playing is only a scratch game, upon the result of which no very great issues hang, to pollute the air they breathe with verbal, and the ground they stand on with physical, buffooneries. Many a time have I, and many a time have you, if you are what I take you for, shed tears of blood, at the sight of such. Careless returns, overthrows—but enough of a painful subject. Let us pass on.

I have always thought it a better fate for a man to be born a bowler than a bat. A batsman certainly gets a considerable amount of innocent fun by snicking good fast balls just off his wicket to the ropes, and standing stolidly in front against slow leg-breaks. These things are good, and help one to sleep peacefully o' nights, and enjoy one's meals. But no batsman can experience that supreme emotion of 'something attempted, something done', which comes to a bowler when a ball pitches in a hole near point's feet, and whips into the leg stump. It is one crowded second of glorious life. Again, the words 'retired hurt' on the score-sheet are far more pleasant to the bowler than the batsman. The groan of a batsman when a loose ball hits him full pitch in the ribs is genuine. But the 'Awfully-sorry-old-chap-it-slipped' of the bowler is not. Half a loaf is better than no bread, as Mr. Chamberlain might say, and if he cannot hit the wicket, he is perfectly contented with hitting the man. In my opinion, therefore, the bowler's lot, in spite of billiard table wickets, red marl, and such like inventions of a degenerate age, is the happier one.

And here, glowing with pride of originality at the thought that I have written of cricket without mentioning Alfred Mynn or Fuller Pilch, I heave a reminiscent sigh, blot my MS., and thrust my pen back into its sheath.

16

THE TOM BROWN QUESTION

The man in the corner had been trying to worry me into a conversation for some time. He had asked me if I objected to having the window open. He had said something rather bitter about the War Office, and had hoped I did not object to smoking. Then, finding that I stuck to my book through everything, he made a fresh attack.

'I see you are reading Tom Brown's Schooldays,' he said.

This was a plain and uninteresting statement of fact, and appeared to me to require no answer. I read on.

'Fine book, sir.'

'Very.'

'I suppose you have heard of the Tom Brown Question?'

I shut my book wearily, and said I had not.

'It is similar to the Homeric Question. You have heard of that, I suppose?'

I knew that there was a discussion about the identity of the author of the Iliad. When at school I had been made to take down notes on the subject until I had grown to loathe the very name of Homer.

'You see,' went on my companion, 'the difficulty about Tom Brown's Schooldays is this. It is obvious that part one and part two were written by different people. You admit that, I suppose?'

'I always thought Mr. Hughes wrote the whole book.'

'Dear me, not really? Why, I thought everyone knew that he only wrote the first half. The question is, who wrote the second. I know, but I don't suppose ten other people do. No, sir.'

'What makes you think he didn't write the second part?'

'My dear sir, just read it. Read part one carefully, and then read part two. Why, you can see in a minute.'

I said I had read the book three times, but had never noticed anything peculiar about it, except that the second half was not nearly so interesting as the first.

'Well, just tell me this. Do you think the same man created East and Arthur? Now then.'

I admitted that it was difficult to understand such a thing.

'There was a time, of course,' continued my friend, 'when

everybody thought as you do. The book was published under Hughes's name, and it was not until Professor Burkett-Smith wrote his celebrated monograph on the subject that anybody suspected a dual, or rather a composite, authorship. Burkett-Smith, if you remember, based his arguments on two very significant points. The first of these was a comparison between the football match in the first part and the cricket match in the second. After commenting upon the truth of the former description, he went on to criticize the latter. Do you remember that match? You do? Very well. You recall how Tom wins the toss on a plumb wicket?'

'Yes.'

'Then with the usual liberality of young hands (I quote from the book) he put the M.C.C. in first. Now, my dear sir, I ask you, would a school captain do that? I am young, says one of Gilbert's characters, the Grand Duke, I think, but, he adds, I am not so young as that. Tom may have been young, but would he, could he have been young enough to put his opponents in on a true wicket, when he had won the toss? Would the Tom Brown of part one have done such a thing?'

'Never,' I shouted, with enthusiasm.

'But that's nothing to what he does afterwards. He permits, he actually sits there and permits, comic songs and speeches to be made during the luncheon interval. Comic Songs! Do you hear me, sir? COMIC SONGS!! And this when he wanted every minute of time he could get to save the match. Would the Tom Brown of part one have done such a thing?'

'Never, never.' I positively shrieked the words this time.

'Burkett-Smith put that point very well. His second argument is founded on a single remark of Tom's, or rather—'

'Or rather,' I interrupted, fiercely,' or rather of the wretched miserable—'

'Contemptible,' said my friend.

'Despicable, scoundrelly, impostor who masquerades as Tom in the second half of the book.'

'Exactly,' said he. 'Thank you very much. I have often thought the same myself. The remark to which I refer is that which he makes to the master while he is looking on at the M.C.C. match. In passing, sir, might I ask you whether the Tom Brown of part one would have been on speaking terms with such a master?'

I shook my head violently. I was too exhausted to speak.

'You remember the remark? The master commented on the fact that Arthur is a member of the first eleven. I forget Tom's exact words, but the substance of them is this, that, though on his merits

123

Arthur was not worth his place, he thought it would do him such a lot of good being in the team. Do I make myself plain, sir? He—thought—it—would—do— him—such—a—lot—of—good—being—in—the—team!!!'

There was a pause. We sat looking at one another, forming silently with our lips the words that still echoed through the carriage.

'Burkett-Smith,' continued my companion, 'makes a great deal of that remark. His peroration is a very fine piece of composition. "Whether (concludes he) the captain of a school cricket team who could own spontaneously to having been guilty of so horrible, so terrible an act of favouritismical jobbery, who could sit unmoved and see his team being beaten in the most important match of the season (and, indeed, for all that the author tells us it may have been the only match of the season), for no other reason than that he thought a first eleven cap would prove a valuable tonic to an unspeakable personal friend of his, whether, I say, the Tom Brown who acted thus could have been the Tom Brown who headed the revolt of the fags in part one, is a question which, to the present writer, offers no difficulties. I await with confidence the verdict of a free, enlightened, and conscientious public of my fellow-countrymen." Fine piece of writing, that, sir?'

'Very,' I said.

'That pamphlet, of course, caused a considerable stir. Opposing parties began to be formed, some maintaining that Burkett-Smith was entirely right, others that he was entirely wrong, while the rest said he might have been more wrong if he had not been so right, but that if he had not been so mistaken he would probably have been a great deal more correct. The great argument put forward by the supporters of what I may call the "One Author" view, was, that the fight in part two could not have been written by anyone except the author of the fight with Flashman in the school-house hall. And this is the point which has led to all the discussion. Eliminate the Slogger Williams episode, and the whole of the second part stands out clearly as the work of another hand. But there is one thing that seems to have escaped the notice of everybody.'

'Yes?' I said.

He leant forward impressively, and whispered. 'Only the actual fight is the work of the genuine author. The interference of Arthur has been interpolated!'

'By Jove!' I said. 'Not really?'

'Yes. Fact, I assure you. Why, think for a minute. Could a man capable of describing a fight as that fight is described, also be

124

capable of stopping it just as the man the reader has backed all through is winning? It would be brutal. Positively brutal, sir!'

'Then, how do you explain it?'

'A year ago I could not have told you. Now I can. For five years I have been unravelling the mystery by the aid of that one clue. Listen. When Mr. Hughes had finished part one, he threw down his pen and started to Wales for a holiday. He had been there a week or more, when one day, as he was reclining on the peak of a mountain looking down a deep precipice, he was aware of a body of men approaching him. They were dressed soberly in garments of an inky black. Each had side whiskers, and each wore spectacles. "Mr. Hughes, I believe?" said the leader, as they came up to him.

'"Your servant, sir," said he.

'"We have come to speak to you on an important matter, Mr. Hughes. We are the committee of the Secret Society For Putting Wholesome Literature Within The Reach Of Every Boy, And Seeing That He Gets It. I, sir, am the president of the S.S.F.P.W.L.W.T.R.O.E.B.A.S.T.H.G.I." He bowed.

'"Really, sir, I—er—don't think I have the pleasure," began Mr. Hughes.

'"You shall have the pleasure, sir. We have come to speak to you about your book. Our representative has read Part I, and reports unfavourably upon it. It contains no moral. There are scenes of violence, and your hero is far from perfect."

'"I think you mistake my object," said Mr. Hughes; "Tom is a boy, not a patent medicine. In other words, he is not supposed to be perfect."

'"Well, I am not here to bandy words. The second part of your book must be written to suit the rules of our Society. Do you agree, or shall we throw you over that precipice?"

'"Never. I mean, I don't agree."

'"Then we must write it for you. Remember, sir, that you will be constantly watched, and if you attempt to write that second part yourself—"' (he paused dramatically). 'So the second part was written by the committee of the Society. So now you know.'

'But,' said I, 'how do you account for the fight with Slogger Williams?'

'The president relented slightly towards the end, and consented to Mr. Hughes inserting a chapter of his own, on condition that the Society should finish it. And the Society did. See?'

'But—'

'Ticket.'

'Eh?'

'Ticket, please, sir.'

I looked up. The guard was standing at the open door. My companion had vanished.

'Guard,' said I, as I handed him my ticket, 'where's the gentleman who travelled up with me?'

'Gentleman, sir? I haven't seen nobody.'

'Not a man in tweeds with red hair? I mean, in tweeds and owning red hair.'

'No, sir. You've been alone in the carriage all the way up. Must have dreamed it, sir.'

Possibly I did.